Tell Me When I Disappear

Vanishing Stories

Tell Me
When I Disappear

Vanishing Stories

Glen Hirshberg

CEMETERY DANCE PUBLICATIONS

Baltimore
❖ 2023 ❖

Cemetery Dance Publications
132B Industry Lane, Unit #7
Forest Hill, MD 21050
www.cemeterydance.com

The characters and events in this book are fictitious.
Any similarity to real persons, living or dead,
is coincidental and not intended by the authors.

Trade Paperback Edition

ISBN:
978-1-58767-868-4

Cover Artwork and Design © 2023 by Lynne Hansen
Cover and Interior Design © 2023 by Desert Isle Design, LLC

For Kae and Sid and Kim:
the way I know I haven't, yet,
and the best reason not to.
With love, always.

Table of Contents

Part One:
...from the land...

Part Two:
...from the Coasts...

Part Three:
...from...

Part One

...from the land...

Black Leg

My fault. As usual.

"Documentary filmmaker," the prosecutor said, not looking at me or any of the other prospective jurors. He wasn't even looking at his legal pad, only the defendant. Even so, everyone in the room felt the weight of his glare. "What sort of documentaries would those be?"

Can prospective jurors plead the Fifth? I wondered. Then I thought maybe in this case the truth really would set me free. "Ghost hunting," I mumbled. "I followed these two—"

"Ghost hunting," said the lawyer. His smile didn't even reach his mouth, let alone his eyes. And it was definitely meant to intimidate me. Or else he was just amused. "So you're not planning to make a film about this case, then?"

There it was: the moment I'd been praying for. He'd practically opened the door for me. Held it, waved me toward freedom and an early, excused return to what passed back then for my life.

But still, he aimed his gaze toward the defendant's table. The terrified kid there, a tousle-haired Latinx with his legs pumping up and down under the table. All that movement barely rippled his billowy jeans, which were three sizes too big, almost certainly some relative's, and made his whole body look like a sack full of cats on its way to the river.

The prosecutor's smirk was for him, of course.

"Why—you seeking the death penalty?" I blurted. "I could make one about him coming back to haunt you."

Which earned me a smirk of my very own, a reprimand from the judge, a lecture to the whole courtroom about the seriousness of our task and the weight of civic responsibility—the case was a contested driving-without-license; the nineteen year-old defendant had run over a birdfeeder, and we didn't know about the sort-of carjacking part yet, or the getaway vehicle element—and, to my dismay, an unchallenged seat and assigned number in the jury box.

The trial, we were told, because of backlogged something or other plus extenuating birdfeeder circumstances, would last four days.

Four days.

That first morning, at lunch break, I thought about braving the heat to find a taco truck or a shake somewhere. But even ghost hunter work had dried up in the recession, and I was hoarding every penny for my long-planned short about the tent city downtown. I had actually completed the raw footage for it, but now the project lingered in seemingly permanent post-production (meaning I still dreamed someone might fund it), and the interest on the credit cards I'd maxed out for my equipment more than doubled my monthly payments.

So I went downstairs to the jury waiting room and bought an apple from the vending machine. It cost seventy-five cents, and got pushed out of its row like a bag of chips. When it hit the metal trough from which I retrieved it, it bounced.

I found an empty table along the back wall, which wasn't hard. Everyone without a maxed-out credit card had fled for anywhere with functioning air conditioning and less aggressive apple delivery, and the remaining prospective jurors took chairs beneath the blaring flat-screen TV at the north end of the room or clustered into the corners, where at least one or two apparently managed—by turning just right, holding still—to get reception on their cell phones.

This room, I remember thinking, the edible half of my mealy apple consumed, right before he appeared. From where would I film it? In what light? I couldn't imagine the angle or the composition. What shot would capture this tile, where even the scuffs had faded, this specific type of fluorescence, which didn't buzz, didn't glow, wasn't even itself? I can't explain. There were bulbs overhead, obviously, but they weren't where the light came from, somehow. Which of these faces best communicated the way all of our faces had gone slack along the jaw, lost some essential shelf of bone that rendered them faces and not masks, collage dots for a future artist's jury box sketch?

We were all doing the same things. Or versions of the same things. Trying to drum up enough brainpower to answer the crossword clue we'd just read four times, or remember what we did for work clearly enough to do some (assuming we could get wireless), or think of anyone or anything in our lives except what we hadn't said (or in my case, had) to get ourselves sentenced here to perform a duty we knew mattered, should care about, just couldn't quite recall why. Not so much passing time as enduring it.

"You make films," the guy said, right at my elbow.

I didn't jump. I don't think I would have remembered how. I did wonder, vaguely, where he'd come from. But I want to be clear: it's true I can't picture his face. But I couldn't have pictured my own, right then.

"Some people call them films," I muttered. Took a bite of the brown side of my apple, feeling all Marlowe. Elliott Gould Marlowe.

"About ghosts."

I took him for Latinx, too, at first. I have a feeling, based on nothing but my own unthinking white person assumptions, that most people do. A little later, before I knew, I decided he was Vietnamese. Maybe Korean. I'm sure it must drive Filipinos crazy.

"I've seen some," he said.

To cover my sigh, I lifted the apple for one more bite, nearly decapitating the tiny no-color worm that poked its head—I kid you not—out of the meat, glanced around like a mini meerkat, then ducked back inside.

Setting the apple on the table, I turned it toward the guy. So the worm could hear, too. I'm pretty sure I gestured at a nearby chair.

The guy just stood there, hands in pockets. His pants were a color, but not one I know a name for. Gabardine? Is that a color a fabric? A color they don't make anymore, anyway. Fabric, either. His shirt was the same. Uniform of some kind. Long-sleeved, in San Fernando, on a 112-degree day.

"One time?" If the guy raised an eyebrow, I didn't see it, wasn't looking. But I actually don't think he moved. "I was working this school? In Van Nuys?"

"What sort of work?" I asked. Automatic impulse. Documenting. Passing time.

"Night."

Right, sure, there's a follow-up question there. But not in that room. Not on an empty stomach. I waited.

"I was walking down this hall? And right behind me, one of the classroom doors? It opened."

I waited some more. I think I even tried to make a noise, I'm not intentionally rude, except to prosecutors with smirks for smiles and my time in their hands. In San Fernando, on 112-degree days.

"Another time?"

Now I really did make a noise, some sort of aural holding up of the palm I couldn't actually bring myself to lift. Protest sound. I mean, if you're going to tell me a ghost story . . .

"I heard this pinging. Ping-ping-ping?"

"In the school?"

"No, at the hospital. There weren't even patients in it anymore, I don't know why they needed night people. Out by Chatsworth?"

"Are you asking me?"

"I heard it. Ping-ping. Out on the stairs? So I went there, and I turned on the lights. And I walked down three flights? And at the bottom, in the basement, I found two little black bug shells. And a penny."

For a second, I was absolutely sure I was being punked. My pal Gabriel, maybe, who specializes in absurdist shorts to sell to comedy cable. Or some stone-faced bailiff secretly delighting himself, because what else would a bailiff with an actual personality do for fun in this place?

"In Pacoima, one time, I was working this lot? Used cars? Behind me, whenever I wasn't looking, headlights flashed on and off."

I felt pinned to my plastic chair, to the whole room, like someone's collected butterfly. Moth, because whatever coloring I possessed had leached away hours ago. Nevertheless, I finally stirred. Flapped.

"If you weren't looking, how did you see them?"

It was a dumb question. It got the answer it deserved.

"They went on. Then off."

Sighing, lifting the apple by its wilted stem and chucking it in the streaked plastic garbage can next to the table, I stood.

"In the same lot, another time? I saw these kids over in the far corner, by Roscoe Street? But on the lot. They saw me, too, and when they did, they moved *toward* me. Then a trash can banged."

I really did think there might be an ending to that one. Or a second episode, anyway. Abruptly, I realized what this whole conversation reminded me of: the world's worst pilot pitch.

"Once?" the guy said. "At the Galleria? I came out of the bathroom on the third floor, and I smelled orange."

"Speaking of the bathroom," I mumbled, gestured at the clock, and made my escape.

He didn't follow. At the door I glanced back. He was still by my table, hands in his pockets. If he was looking at anything, it was the chair where I'd been sitting. I felt bad. I waved.

The second I was out of there, though, I forgot feeling bad about anything except being trapped here for the rest of the week. I was going to have to find a shade tree somewhere not in the jury room. Bring my own apples. I stayed in the bathroom stall until it was time to be readmitted to court.

They only kept us another hour, that day. Long enough to finish voir dire. I'd forgotten to look for my lunch companion, and I honestly believe I might never have thought of him again. But right at the end, when the judge was getting ready to have the bailiff install us, the prosecutor glanced up from his notes. No smirk. He looked as tired and trapped as the rest of us.

"The prosecution wishes to thank and excuse Alternate Number Two."

There was no ado or fuss. The judge did raise one eyebrow, and the defense attorney dropped a hand to his table as though preparing to object. But he didn't, and the moment rippled through the room and out of it. At the left-hand end of the jury box, my lunch companion stood, brushed his hands against his pants, opened his mouth. Maybe just to breathe. Nothing came out. He didn't shrug. Just moved, head down, out of the box. In the silent whoosh of air as he passed under the room's lone vent, his shirt bubbled, and his collar—half turned wrong way out, stained black where it touched his skin—bristled against his neck. Down the little aisle he went.

Even the Latinx kid, led out in handcuffs at trial's end three days later, looked less forlorn.

Maybe that's why I did it. Maybe that's why I remembered the guy at all.

All I know is, a couple weeks later, I was sitting at my tilting apartment kitchen table—which was also my desk—confronting reality. The amateur-hour paranormal series that had paid me a semi-living for three years running had given up the ghost. My last-ditch Kickstarter for my tent city doc had gotten two pledges, one each from my mom and step-aunt. My step-aunt had suggested—in the public comments, on the web page—that I offer "more practical" premiums as pledge rewards: bar mitzvah or wedding videos, say. Or yard work.

Yard work.

I could have taken the comment down. But something about my week in court—the terrified defendant, the inexorability of the case, the decision we were all helpless to avoid by the end, even though it seemed absurd, draconian, laughable except for being the opposite of funny—had put me in a confronting-reality sort of mood.

Unexpectedly, I thought about my lunch companion. Not our conversation, not anything he'd said, but him passing in front of the jury box with his head down, collar bristling. Thanked and excused. Not necessary. I realized I didn't even know his name.

I had to put down my half-peeled orange to grab my phone. Maybe that's what actually possessed me: I smelled orange.

Funny word, *possessed*.

The collar, it turned out, wasn't the only thing I remembered about the guy's shirt. I could also see the name, stitched in red cursive over the pocket. Not the guy's name, but his company's.

Look Outs, Inc.

I don't remember thinking it was funny—the two words instead of one—in the court room. But it seemed funny, now, the first thing all month I'd laughed about. It also seemed…I don't know. Sweet. How condescending is that?

Anyway, I laughed. Then I looked up *Look Outs, Inc.*, and called them.

The phone call was also hilarious. The first one, anyway. *Um, yeah, I don't actually know his name. But he's worked at, let me think, a hospital, a school, and a used car lot. Yes, I understand those are all places you staff. At night, he does nights. Which, ah, that's your whole business, got it. All over the whole city, huh? Valleys, too? Good for you.*

For my second call, I led with, "He sees ghosts."

Occupational hazard, the bubbly woman on the other end of the line assured me. I was about to hang up, give up, when she suddenly said, "Wait, Bulan? Our friendly Filipino? Do you mean Bulan?"

"Erm…yes? Did he have jury duty a couple weeks ago?"

Which is how I found myself, GoPro riding shotgun, speeding up the 5 into the never-ending mall that is Santa Clarita, California, at one in the morning on an August Tuesday night. There was a moon, big and fat and orange. For LA on the lip of fire season, the sky seemed stunningly clear. By which I mean the city lights seemed to reflect off it, as though from the mirrored underside of a dome. One of those lights really was Venus, though. I'm pretty sure.

"You'll never find him," the woman had assured me. Good-naturedly.

"Didn't you just give me the address?"

"You been up there?"

Step-aunt lived there. I knew what she meant.

"Does he have a walkie-talkie or something?"

"A what? Why?"

"For…you know, night watchman business. What if he sees something?"

"He calls the cops."

"Not the office?"

"Some of us have homes," the bubbly woman said. That seemed less good-natured, somehow.

It really did take more than an hour, even after I'd gotten on the right never-ending frontage road, to locate the place. On one side of the street, malls and mall parking lots fanned forever like a trick deck of cards, Gap-Vans-Guess-Boss-AmericanEagle-TrueReligion-BananaRepublic. Pull in anywhere, tap any card, you get Food Court. "Look for the Starbucks," the bubbly woman had said. Twenty minutes into my search, at the moment I was closest to sure I'd already passed what I was passing even though I'd neither turned nor turned around, I realized that had been a joke. A pretty good one.

On the other side of the street, identical faux-rock formations framed signs for subdivisions. Porter Canyon. Golden Horse Hills. The Oaks, where my step-aunt lived. The Oaks again. Unless it was the same Oaks, with separate entrances. Or the same entrance, and I'd looped somehow. My car didn't have GPS, and as usual, I'd forgotten my phone—in those days, at one fifteen in the morning, who would I have called?—but at some point I started imagining and mouthing directions.

"You have reached your—wait—in two hundred and fifty feet, turn ar—you have reached your…recalculating route . . ."

What neither the buildings nor the subdivision signs had were numbers. A few times, I saw painted addresses over storm drains fronting the wide, brilliantly lit, sidewalks. All of them were within a few hundred of the number I'd been given, some above, some below. None were the number I wanted. The only other vehicles I passed were cop cars. Or the same cop car. Always, every time, headed the other direction, no matter which direction I was going. Always at the same speed, like a duck on tracks in a shooting gallery.

I almost gave up and went home. Even now, I can't say what told me I'd found it. I think I pulled into the lot to turn around and head back to the freeway, which was always nearby, a traffic light and on-ramp away, as though I'd stayed tethered to it, trotted beside it all this time like its pet. *Californians*, I remember thinking. *Freeway pets.*

Facing the buildings, I saw the same stores on either side of the entrance. Vans, Banana, Levis. Starbucks, haha, get you a frap, Madame Look Out? Then I realized there was an unmarked building between them. Long, low, stretching like a hangar way back into…not darkness, obviously, they've rounded up the darkness and put it in shelters in Santa Clarita.

But distance.

I'm sure half those malls have office complexes or structures like this one tucked into them. But somehow—by its facelessness, its emptiness, its, I don't know, hands-in-pockets humility—I knew this was the place.

Market Circle Business Centre. With an -re.

Did I ever actually see a sign that said that? Confirmed my guess? Was Market Circle Business Centre even that specific building's name, and not just a designation, like East Wing or Restrooms? Why do I still, even now, avoid thinking about how I knew?

Instinctively, I parked near the front of the empty, endless lot, but not *at* the front. A good ten spaces away. I wasn't nervous. I wasn't anything. Those front spaces, though…They just aren't where one parks. Not without the company of other cars.

As I got out, though, stepped into motionless air that was fresher than any I'd breathed in months but tasted recirculated, not so much stale as deoxygenated, I heard my jury room lunch companion's voice. Not on the breeze, not spectrally. In my memory, where it belonged: *I heard this pinging. Ping-ping-ping?*

Otherwise, I just heard silence. The suburb-built-on-desert kind, suspended over fifty-mile sidewalks next to deserted malls.

As I crossed the lot, a cop car passed, but on my side of the street this time. I don't know what made seeing it so alarming, but I almost dove back into my own car. If I'd done so, I think I might also have hid.

Why? No idea. I couldn't see the officer through the vehicle's darkened windows, and anyway, I was probably a football field away from the street.

Maybe the cop didn't see me. Maybe I looked like even less of a threat than I felt, to anything or anyone anywhere.

The cop car passed. I shouldered my GoPro, and with no particular apprehension, no specific feeling at all except a wave of exhaustion, stepped over the little curb, out of the parking lot and into the mall.

For the next…I don't actually know how long, but I was back in my car, fleeing and weeping, by two twenty. So. Thirty minutes? Less? All I did in the time I spent there was walk the mall. The Market Circle Business Centre ran all the way down the middle of it like some sort of breakwater—break-air—and so I wandered around it, looking for a way in, or lights, or a door on which to knock. I flicked on the GoPro a couple times and filmed my shoes.

More than anything, I felt like I was traversing a soundstage. Or down-town Disney. Some places—schools, office complexes, even other malls—feel eerie with no one in them, because it always feels like there *should* be someone in them, right? Or has been, moments before. But these Southern California sidewalk worlds…they feel eerie because the thousands of people who pass through them leave no trace. The sidewalks are always spotless, the windows free of fingerprints. The buildings don't even feel anchored to the land. More like something assembled on Minecraft and projected. About as suggestive of current, active habitation as flags on the moon.

At one point, passing a shuttered Ann Taylor outlet, I took a turn around the back of the Business Centre, and the actual moon blazed down on me like a lighthouse beam. It hung there, seemingly right at the end of this row of shops, gigantic, ridiculous. As fake as everything else in Santa Clarita. An emoji moon pasted onto what passed out there for blackness.

I almost returned to my car. I felt ridiculous. Instead, I pointed my GoPro straight into the light and kept going, figuring sooner or later I'd find a door to knock on, a way into the Business Centre. When I lowered my cam-era, I glanced right, wanting a glimpse of my own reflection in the window glass just to confirm I was actually there, and saw a woman.

She was just standing in the center aisle of the Foot Locker outlet, which wasn't dark, had to have had at least some lights on. She was old, or older:

white curly hair, pince-nez, some kind of dark-colored necklace that seemed to trap light more than reflect it. The little beads weren't uniform, looked mottled or cracked.

Like beetle shells, I remember thinking as I passed. I didn't stop moving, barely had time to process. But somehow, I noted the necklace. And the way the woman had her arms folded across her chest. She was holding a pair of blue Skechers. Also, she was crying.

It didn't even seem strange. Not right away. Why shouldn't she be in there, straightening, restocking?

In a beetle necklace. Crying.

I glanced back in her direction. Just as I did, the store lights went out. In the instant *after* I saw her face, which was right at the window, pressed hard against the glass so her nose slid sideways.

That stopped me. Held me pinned to that placeless place.

I laughed.

"And right behind me, one of the classroom doors? It opened . . ."

Turning my attention back to Business Centre, I focused again on finding an entrance. Eventually I did, around the far side, where this wing of shops emptied into yet another acre of parking lot: one door, heavy, metallic, and locked.

Had I seen even a single window in the Business Centre before then? Why not? What could the dedicated workers who presumably staffed this place possibly be doing in there, and why do it in the middle of the mall?

There was a moment, right around then, when I thought I might have stumbled onto something. A film the Kickstarter crowd might actually fund, and incidentally get my tent city project out of post-production in the process.

I knocked on the door.

Desert breeze kicked up, surprisingly strong, whipping across me and into the mall behind me. Past the Foot Locker outlet. In my mind—*only in my mind*, I did not see this—the old woman lifted away, tumbling over the sidewalks and out of sight like a plastic bag.

The second time I knocked, I got an answer. From behind me.

I don't even remember the sound, couldn't begin to tell you what it was, am not even sure there *was* sound; it could have been vibration underground. A temblor, they happen all the time out there, never really stop, as though the whole planet has Parkinson's, is slowly shuddering itself and us to pieces.

So maybe I just felt, didn't hear. Maybe it wasn't in response to my knock at all.

Whatever. I was too busy whirling, fumbling my GoPro up to my face and turning it on—from protective instinct, not directorial—and so I saw what I saw through the lens.

I've played the footage back a thousand times since then. I still can't say. Neither can anyone I've shown it to. Is that a dragonfly passing? Wrong-color hummingbird? What you see is what I saw: a streak of black in the air, right at eye level, like a smear on the lens itself.

Or a contrail.

Behind me, the door knocked.

Real sound, not vibration; I definitely heard it. I didn't whirl—I'll admit it, was afraid to, scared I'd find *old woman face pressing right into mine with her breath in my nose, in my mouth*—but I turned. Slowly. Lowering the GoPro, mostly because I'd lost my sense of how close I was to the door and didn't want to bang it.

The door banged. Much louder. Four knocks, rapid-fire, *rat-a-tat-tat*.

I did what you do when someone knocks, what instinct and civilization has trained us to do: I reached out my hand. Right before I touched metal, the door *drummed*. *Pound-pound-pound*, double-fisted, surely. I kept expecting the metal to shudder in its frame, but it was heavy, thick, gave no visible sign.

Hoisting the GoPro again, I got it almost to my face, felt more than saw movement to my left, darted my eyes that direction.

She was maybe fifteen feet away. The woman with the necklace. Except it was a different woman. Same necklace, totally different person. Young, black hair in a ponytail, blouse and shiny shirt-vest bright pink. Skechers blue, and on her feet. Less *Ringu* monster than K-pop star. At least until the necklace twitched. Shuddered to life all at once, like plugged-in Christmas lights. The shells sprouted legs.

The moon switched off.

I wasn't consciously filming, wasn't even thinking, just recording sensation in my brain. But where did the light come from? How did I see the coyote?

They're fair questions. I can't answer them.

It loped out of the Restrooms corridor right at the end of the mall across the sidewalk from me. It didn't trot toward the woman, didn't yip or bare its teeth. It just stood, working its mangy mouth, which dripped. The least surprising living thing there, really. Assuming it *was* living. And actually there.

Wind whipped up again, too hot for the night, hotter than the air should have been, and it reeked. Dead skunk. Breath mint. Old orange.

I wasn't thinking any of those things, then. They're what I've pieced together since. Or, right, maybe invented. When I'm in comfort-myself mode, I decide I invented it.

Because otherwise, that reek was combined breath: The coyote's; the woman's/women's; and her beetles'.

The ground buzzed like a cell phone receiving messages. Or a million seventeen-year locusts erupting out of the Earth all at once. I looked down, staggered sideways. The coyote humped up, slunk to its left, but closer. Circling me. Hemming me in. Or herding me toward the woman, who'd gone old again, though still in the K-pop vest. Her necklace seethed on her collarbone like crabs on rock.

Or one big crab.

I turned to run, wasn't even considering which direction, and finally noticed the Business Centre door.

The open door.

Everything stopped. It was pitch black inside, or at least I thought so at first. In retrospect, though, that moment was like the first glance up past streetlights into night sky. It takes a while. What we like to call stars coming out is really just our eyes adjusting. Finally seeing what's there.

Still. There definitely weren't any lights *on* inside. Just a hallway, long and shadowed. Doors took shape, all of them windowless, all of them closed. A water fountain. And then, way down at the end—or not the end, maybe just at the lip of even darker shadows—I spotted my guy. Bulan.

Even in the jury assembly room, even while he was talking, I'd barely bothered to look at his face. I recognized him now by his slump. The fit of his uniform shirt. Same one, I was sure. He had a flashlight in one hand, not switched on. Half-peeled banana in the other.

Did he recognize me? Even today, I wonder. Do they allow him recognition?

In the most mournful, pathetic way—as though at the window of a plunging plane—he lifted the banana and waved.

I stepped into the Business Centre, started forward, and a curl of shadow, like a stray black hair, rose out of his collar and burrowed along his neck. The shadow had bristles. A spider leg. Beetle leg. Same as the legs sprouting from the old woman's shell necklace, seething in place rather than crawling.

Not beetles, I realized. Not crabs.

Ticks.

Somehow, I kept myself moving forward. At least until I saw the rest of them:

Streaks of black filled the air between us. A woman—that woman? One of them? Both?—shimmered into existence, blinked out, blazed back again. The coyote appeared—just its mouth, then its tail, its slinky shoulders—hovering. Hunching in place. There/not-there/there. All of it swirling maybe halfway down the hall like an eddy in a river, with more black streaks radiating from it, swirling off it like mist. Right before the whole thing balled together—coiled—I realized it wasn't like a river at all. It was too contained. Too *intentional.*

More of a moat.

It exploded toward me. Coyote/women/bristle-shadow legs, and I dropped the GoPro, stumbled, grabbed the GoPro, and ran.

Left Bulan there. Ran.

Not because I'm a coward. Not only. They weren't…after him. Or they already had him. To the extent I thought anything, that's what I thought.

I think it still.

I wonder if he even saw them. If, for him, it was always more like looking up from the bottom of a pool. Seeing lights flicker. Hearing pings.

I don't remember sprinting to my car. I don't remember wind, light, sound, shaking earth, anything. I don't remember the drive. Somehow, I wound up on my step-aunt's porch up in The Oaks, clutching the cocoa she'd made me, babbling at her as she sat in her robe and bare feet on her porch swing and stared out at the identical houses across the way and around her. At some point, for some reason, I heard myself talking about my uncle, who'd refused morphine all the way to the end, and died screaming so loudly that we could hear him all the way down in the family waiting area. I was describing winces and tears on nurse's faces. One nurse in particular, a young one, Elysia, who'd always smiled at my step-aunt and put a hand on her shoulder.

I didn't know about the Diwata yet. I learned about them later, on one of those days when this all resurfaced. By then, I'd given up trying to find Bulan—he'd quit, I'd been told, vanished, no one even seemed to have a record of his last name—and instead just rooted around hopelessly on the internet. The Diwata are Filipino fairies. Or a Tagalog name, anyway, for fairies who spirit you away. Claim you for their own. Won't let you leave.

Were they what I saw? How would I even begin to know?

The only thing I know is Bulan's raised hand, holding banana. Those slumped shoulders. *The prosecution wishes to thank and excuse.* My lonely step-aunt, and that nurse touching her shoulder. The people and moments that attach to us as we pass like ticks, burrow in, make us sick, separate us, but also, just maybe, form the only reliable bridge we'll ever have between ourselves and anyone else. Their hard shells the path we traverse on our way through woods we all walk to someone else's porch, so we can sit and tell the story of how we got there.

Devil

All the way back to the Conservancy Center, Tim kept the van windows cracked open despite the cold and the drumming rain. "So you can hear," he told the Americans in the back, and watched them all—father, mother, kids—swivel to the nearest windows to stare hard into the Tasmanian dark. Already, Tim knew, they were reframing those moments even as they relived them. Embalming and enshrining them. Turning them into stories.

From the passenger seat, Mika caught his eye, wrapped her arms tight to herself. Didn't wink, might as well have. At the end of tour-days like this, when they'd actually glimpsed one back there in the bush, when the woods seethed with weather and all that life they hid, and the tourists who'd hired them were interested and ready to be wowed, Mika was practically a walking wink.

Except…how many tour-days like this had there been, *lately? When was the last time they'd even spotted a devil in the wild? Let alone one with whatever it had just devoured still dripping from its jaws?*

Was it just the devil sighting that had created those last moments? That sense of the woods shifting around them, tricking them, turning into other woods, so that the third time the teenaged boy asked Mika if she was positive *this was the way they'd come—which, sure, was mostly just an excuse for him to talk and walk next to Mika some more—even Tim had found himself holding his breath. Awaiting her answer.*

Which had turned out to be a laugh. Possibly even a nervous one. Instead of 'yes'.

Which had led him to increase their pace, more than he'd realized. So that at the end—the path clearly their path, now, the van not quite visible but less than 100 meters away—at the exact moment son, then daughter, then mom and dad had all started sprinting, Tim had barely had to speed up. He'd watched them run, flinging glances over their shoulders like spent rocket fuel, watched Mika charging in front of him, watched her *glance back, felt himself do it, saw trees and shrubs surging in the whistling wind and whipping rain, and further back, up on the hill, the taller trees tipping almost all the way over as if crouching to take wing, as if the whole forest was about to lift off and flee, or else swoop down and take them. When he'd dropped the keys trying to click the van open, lost and then fumbled for them momentarily in the underbrush, even Mika had wheeled on him, snapping, "Oh, beauty, Tim, COME on!" before grabbing the family's gear to hurl it into the back.*

Actual wild moments. His wildest in years.

For Mika, too. He'd seen it in her face, though he knew her well enough to suspect she was already in the process of reclassifying. Denying.

"Sssh," she whispered now to the tourists. To the boy who whipped his head around to her. "Listen."

Recognizing his cue, Tim slid the Fabulous Diamonds CD into the deck. The music, would of course drown out any actual forest sounds that the van motor didn't. And yet. Played way down low, these tracks perfectly accentuated these nights. Rumbled and rolled like the road beneath them, amplified. Gave a beat to the rattling rain. Transformed the sighing wind caught in the window openings into black kites, keening.

Most nights, he played this music to sustain the Tassie-ness of the day for the tourists. But tonight, it was also weirdly comforting. It settled and slowed his heart.

Still shuddering, the boy glanced from the window to Mika and back, gape-mouthed as a five year-old.

She's not even pretty, Tim marveled for the thousandth time, and for once, he was absolutely sure this wasn't just their year-old breakup talking.

Coiled there with her knees to her chest and her muddy boots caking new layers of sludge atop the caked sludge on her seat, wet-dirt hair whipping around and across her round, freckled face, she really did look like some sort of dwarf pine, stumpy and solid, the laughter erupting from somewhere way down inside her like bird call. As though Mika wasn't her body at all, but a wild thing nested in it.

"Should we?" she stage-whispered, to Tim.

Tired, he was about to say, swerving suddenly as a wallaby materialized just ahead, eyes glinting in the headlights. He stayed on the wrong side of the road to avoid the already-dead thing humped a few hundred feet further ahead, body curled neatly in on itself like raked leaves. Possum, possibly. By the time he remembered Mika's question, he'd missed his moment.

"When we get back," she was already saying. Addressing the parents, hardly even glancing at the boy. Having herself a grand Mika time doing that. "You want to come along to the Den? Join us for a beer and a slice? To celebrate?"

"Slice of what?" the mother asked, and Tim smiled to himself.

"Slice. It's like cake."

"Damn right!" the boy said immediately. But not as fast as his mother, who clapped her hands and thanked them.

Which made Tim like this whole group all over again. Mika, too, and why not? They'd gotten along all week. They had a proper Roaring Forty windstorm blasting and juddering around them outside the van, the Fabulous Diamonds on the radio, a night alive with eyes and rain. And they'd seen a free-roaming devil, bloody-mouthed and scurrying half up a tree before turning its face on them: ears pricked, deceptive teddy-bear eyes wide. No tumors ballooning from its cheeks. Cuddle-thing cute in the second before it yawned, opened those still-healthy jaws and went on opening, the teeth seemingly studded all the way down its throat like piercings, like the teeth of the trees themselves, and they'd all shivered in place, held still. Not one of them even saw for sure where it went, whether up or around back or down into the ground or the brush. Which meant they'd gotten not only an actual devil sighting but that delicious before-we-had-brains dread of being stalked.

Which, Tim thought, *was almost certainly what the devil had experienced, too. Startled surprise. Then dread.*

Did devils dread?

One thing was certain: he himself apparently still did. And that was *before* they'd all lit out running for the van.

A night worth celebrating, for sure, now they were safely out of it.

"How about a game 'til we get there?" Tim heard himself say, and caught Mika's surprised grin out of the corner of his eye. Sexiest thing about her. Rare as a devil sighting when they were alone, now. Which was almost never, anyway.

"You know the license plate game?" Mika asked the family, falling right into their old rhythm.

"Don't you need other cars for that?" murmured the dad from the back.

It was, Tim realized, the first sentence the guy had spoken since they'd returned to the van. He'd spent the whole ride staring into the dark. Taking it in. Settling his nerves. Or stealing some rare family vacation musing time. Either way, Tim liked him. Good family, this.

"Right, mate. This one's the Tassie version." Automatically, he swerved again to avoid the next carcass on the asphalt ahead. It always unnerved him, the way wallabies seemingly stretched out as they got hit, or in the split second before they got hit. As though prostrating themselves. In the road, when they were dead, their corpses looked laid out like meat on a table. Ready for carving.

Mika explained the rules. One point per roadkill spotted.

"High scoring game," the dad murmured.

Which meant he really had been paying attention. Tim nodded even though he didn't think the guy could see him. "There's still a lot of life out here."

"Dead life."

"Same thing."

"Annnd he's back. Have-a-Whinge Tim," Mika chirped, then stuck out her tongue in the old, pre-breakup way. The way where she still liked him. Where he still liked himself with her.

Apparently, both things held true tonight. Devil-magic. Post-dread comradeship.

"*Two* points if you spot something alive in time for Tim to avoid it."

"Extra points if you can name the species," said Tim, swerving for fun, and the mom and son yelped, and the daughter grinned, and the dad caught his eye in the rearview. Shared a dad moment with him, even if Tim wasn't one. Which felt nice. "Possum's worth one point. Wallabies are two."

"Birds three," Mika said, primarily so the son back there could say, *Birds?*, which he promptly did. "Lot of birds out here, mate."

"What about a devil?" the mom asked abruptly. Apprehensively. In a way that suggested she understood just how awful and stupid that would be, given the whole island's—the whole nation's—conservation efforts, the attempts to wall off and save this last, wild remnant from the face cancer devouring the entire species.

Tim nodded appreciation at her. "Negative points. Happens a lot, unfortunately. They're carrion eaters first, remember. This highway's like a 100-kilometer buffet table for a devil."

Another swerve, real this time, the wallaby already dead but still unfurling into its legs-outstretched corpse pose, as though the accident had just happened even though Tim hadn't seen a single other vehicle coming or going since returning to the van. As though whatever had hit it had fallen on it with the rain.

"Platypus, ten," said Mika, and both parents started guffawing, then stopped when Mika just stared at them. "Think I'm kidding? Am I kidding, Tim?"

"Sadly not. After rains like this, lots of times, they come right up out of the creeks."

There was a silence. The glorious Tassie kind, wind howling and rain drumming and the Diamonds churning and melting in the speakers like magma. Then the daughter yelled, "Wallaby!", and Tim swerved, and Mika awarded her two points and held out her hand for a down-low slap.

A long time later—they were almost back, the ground rising as the trees fell away, the space between dead things elongating as the numbers of invisible live things out there declined—the boy stirred in the back. He'd been obliterated by his sister in the game, and Tim had taken his silence for sullenness. But the wonder (and at least a little of the fear) was still in his voice when he spoke, and he kept straining against his seat belt to get a last look back the way they'd come. There was something endearing, childlike about the way he did that. Tim half-expected him to wave.

"What about people?" he asked.

"People?" The sister settled back in her seat, regal in triumph. "Mom, he's doing the babbling thing."

"Do people ever get hit out here? It's so dark."

To his own surprise, Tim felt himself grin. He modulated his voice, slowed his cadence. Even to himself, he sounded uncannily like the Old Damper from the Den. Mika had always teased that Tim would one day become the Damper. Assume his mantle, live out his days camped in a folding chair in that room's back corner, waiting for tour groups to come in from the brush so he could tell them stories. Right then, in the van, there seemed worse fates. "Do people get hit? Na, mate. People just disappear."

There it was again: the shared dad-thing glance with the father. The mother laughing, the kids, too. He half-turned to Mika for the wink he'd surely earned.

But Mika had her lips pursed, her gaze in the sideview mirror, aimed behind them. Back the way they'd come. After a hesitation so slight it might not even have been one, she shrugged.

Five minutes later, the streetlamps surrounding the low, cement buildings of the Conservation Visitor Center swam up in the windshield, bleary and flickering, as though projected from an old Super-8. For the first time in ages, Tim felt a twinge of disappointment. Like when he'd just been ordered out of his childhood community pool in Brisbane so the adults could swim laps. Playtime over.

Because the wild really had been wild, today. And they'd seen a devil, for the first time in almost a year.

"Could you all check to make sure any headlamps or thermoses or gear we lent you gets stored with the rest in the back?" he asked as he parked next to the Conservancy's three other vans in the corner of the lot. "Mika will check you out. Then we'll lead you around back to the Den."

"For your secret celebration slice," Mika said, and *now* she winked, not at Tim but the poor kid back there. Her freckles seemed to blaze from her face like little meteors.

Quite a night this kid was having.

The rain hadn't lightened, but the wind slackened at least temporarily. The family all danced and shivered beside the van as backpacks and ponchos got sorted and checkout forms signed, but neither Mika nor Tim so much as bothered wiping wetness out of their eyes. Point of pride, and also habit. Weather like this barely qualified as storm, here. Rolled through and down them as though they were trees.

"Right." Slamming the back door shut, Tim gestured around the side of the Visitor Center. "Denward."

They were maybe three steps from the van when the shriek erupted.

It poured down from the hillsides beyond the buildings, but also bubbled up from the tarmac, the echo almost preceding the sound, the whole thing curling over itself like a wave breaking. It just kept coming, too. In the end, it didn't so much die as shut itself off like a kettle removed from heat. Or a hawk having struck.

"*What?*" the father hissed, frozen mid-step the way they all were, and hunched, too. As though hunted. About to be. Tim thought again of that unfurling wallaby in the road they'd just traversed.

Even Mika looked right at him. Mouthed, *Wow.*

Mother and daughter had thrown their arms around each other, but now the daughter shook free, raked rain out of her hair as she stared past the Center into the dark beyond it. "You have the most amazing birds, here."

Mika's answer was immediate, dictated by the tone of this whole day, the nature of this specific guided group. Plus the fact that she was Mika.

"We do." Beat. "But that wasn't one of them."

"*Drop bear!*" the son shouted, and his sister shoved him.

"Not real."

Even as he waved everyone forward, Tim had to give the whole family credit, again. Not a single one of them had hunched into their jackets or whined about cold or wetness. The parents, in particular, were clinging to this night. Imprinting all of it—devil, Roaring Forty, Fabulous Diamonds, Tassie dark, terrifying mystery shriek, their children, everything but Tim and Mika—into memory.

"Now, think," Mika was teasing. Flirting. Though even she kept stealing glances toward the hills. "Why would a drop bear make that sound?"

"To claim territory," the boy said immediately. "Alert anything and everything about who's boss."

"Thereby defeating the whole purpose of being a drop bear, yeah? Lot easier to drop out of a tree onto someone's back if they never know you're there."

By now, they'd reached the overhang, and the sister's laughter reverberated down the paved breezeway between concrete buildings. Tim gestured toward the restrooms, and all four family members broke off, leaving him and Mika alone for just a moment under the tin roof, in the drumming rain, looking at each other through the shadowy dark. Which is how they had always seen each other. Would always. It was the way *they* were imprinted.

"They're cute," he said, gesturing toward the laughter echoing out of the restrooms.

To his surprise, Mika reached up and brushed a wet curl off his forehead. "You, too. Sometimes."

"You three," he murmured.

"Hey, Tim?" She glanced down the breezeway, out the opening at the far end toward the back lot. "What *was* that?"

The family returned. The sister cut in front the boy, marched right up to Tim. "Please tell him, once and for all, there's no such thing as a drop bear."

Pressing his lips together, Tim shrugged. "Do not mock the drop. But… hey, what's that on your shoulder?" Lunging past the sister, he made a furious sweep at the son's jacket. The kid flinched, stumbled back.

"That's not funny," he snapped, while his sister laughed.

"Not laughing, mate. Never mind drop bears. We have spiders here that could chew your arm right off."

Mika joined in immediately. "Octopi as small as your palm that can shut down your whole neuro-system with one sucker-touch." She stuck out a finger, and the daughter ducked back.

"Let us not neglect the poor, hounded Tasmanian Devil," Tim said, leading them down the breezeway. "Which, as we informed you before, literally devours entire corpses, of any kind, the second it finds them. Hair, bones, teeth, cellphones, pocket watches, you name it. And it does so in a frenzy so violent that if there are two of them doing it, they will bite *through each other's faces* and just keep right on eating. Which, poor cute devils, is part of the reason we are having so much trouble containing the disease that may literally exterminate them. They're not model quarantine citizens."

As if on cue, the wind kicked up, plastering their wet clothes against their already soaked skins. Even Tim and Mika shivered, wrapped their arms to their chests and moved more quickly toward the Den.

"They'd really eat a cellphone?" the dad murmured.

"In a heartbeat. Without a thought, if they have thoughts."

"What if they break their teeth?"

"Wouldn't even slow them down."

"Then there's the giant carnivorous snail," Mika said, and they rounded the corner around back of the Center, which got them out of the worst of the wind but set the resurgent rain raking over them.

"Okay," laughed the mother, huddling into her son, "I'm calling drop bear on giant carnivorous snails."

"I'm calling stupid," said the boy, and Mika waggled a finger at him.

"You'd be wrong. They're not *so* giant, I admit, and you actually find them on the mainland. But they *are* carnivorous. You should never, ever doubt. Not in Australia. Especially not on Tassie."

"Except about drop bears," the sister mumbled.

The door to the Den had no peephole, no handle or knob, just a bolt lock that didn't actually have a bolt in it as far as Tim knew. Not one anybody used, anyway. Even as he pushed open the door and stood aside to shepherd everyone in, he marveled again at the effect this place had on him. On everyone. In his mind, the place had a hazy, smoky, firelit glow; in reality, there was no fireplace, not even any light fixtures, just bare bulbs in a straight track down the center of the low ceiling. No posters, no wallpaper. Concrete walls, a few scattered circular white plastic tables with a handful of folding chairs circulating amongst them as trail groups or group leaders came in, pumped themselves cups of reheated coffee or homemade pumpkin soup from the thermoses on the craft services table, grabbed a slice from under the Cling-wrap on the tray Swannie or his ma always dropped off in the morning. Mostly caramel, those slices, though sometimes chocolate mint. Rarely any variations beyond those. The place was really more airplane hangar than pub or even break room. A people-garage.

"Hey," the mother said as she passed Tim. Her family was already across the room, accepting plastic cups and spoons as Mika doled them out, the dad elbowing his son aside and laughing as he unwrapped the slice tray and grabbed a paper plate. She gestured toward the back wall, but Tim knew she was really thinking about the hills out there. The whistling downpour. Same as him. "Do you know what kind of bird that was? For real?"

"Are you joking?" said the Damper from his corner, and both Tim and the mom startled, whirled around.

There he sat where he always sat when he was here. Which hadn't been so often, lately. He'd been sick, word had it. Sick*er*. The gravel in his voice box running riot down his throat, through his glands.

He also looked genuinely surprised to see them. Alarmed, almost. He cleared his throat, and his too-prominent Adam's apple bobbed under his thin skin like something he'd just swallowed.

"You weren't really out there, Tim?"

The question surprised him. "It's just rain, Damper."

"You didn't have *them* out there?"

"You appear to be out here."

"I'm *in here*. For the company."

Glancing around the room, just to make sure he hadn't missed something as they entered, Tim nodded. Felt a ping of free-floating sadness. "The joint is jumpin'."

Judging by the crumb-strewn plates in front of him, the Damper was well into slice number three. His Dodges Ferry football jumper looked ridiculous on him, at least three sizes too big, the giant red shark logo seemingly just burst from his ribs. The beanie on his head was even more ridiculous, its fire-red cross logo tilted and glowing over his left eye, as though he'd just been branded.

"Jesus, Damper. Who bought *you* a Dark MOFO hat?"

The Damper was still staring at him out of those perpetually leaking, yellowy eyes. Cat eyes. Finally, he shrugged. "Everyone on the booking committee got one."

Never failed. Tim felt his jaw unhinge. Half drop, half slip sideways in the direction of grinning. "*You* were on the Dark MoFo booking committee."

From across the room, Mika burst into laughter. "Surprised, Tim? You know a darker mofo? Excluding your own fine self, of course."

"What's a dark mofo?" the sister asked, and the dad started to shush her, and Tim waved him off.

"It's a...actually, it's kind of hard to describe. An arts and music festival."

"But dark," Mika added.

"Like...death metal?"

"Yeah. No. Sometimes. It's a Tassie thing. In a kind of...new-old way. Pagan. Performance art. There's *some* death metal, most years. Also really, really good food. And some..." Finally, Tim gave up. Ceded the Damper the drop-mouthed grin he apparently craved. "Ask him. He apparently books it."

"Ask me anything you like," said the Damper. "Just be sure you want to know."

The Damper was not grinning. Mostly, he was still staring at Tim. The pallor of his cheeks was probably illness. The shake of the head might have been tremors.

Did the Damper have tremors?

If he did, Tim had never noticed them. Given how many nights they'd spent together in the past three years, it was amazing how little Tim knew about the Damper, except that he came here ridiculously often, as though the Den were an actual pub. Soup and coffee and slices poured down him. Words spilled from him. As though he were a record player, almost. Console radio. Thing in the corner that you switched on, settled near, and listened to. Not always for comfort, just because it was there.

That's how they all treated him, Tim realized. And now here was his own sadness again.

And *still*, the Damper was staring at Tim.

It was the son, surprisingly, who skipped them past the moment they'd apparently gotten stuck in. Not only set down a plate and cup for himself but brought one of each, unasked, to the Damper. For the first time, the old man seemed to notice him. He nodded at the kid in what Tim first thought was thanks, then snapped, "Hear it?"

The kid glanced toward his mom, then Tim. Then the ceiling. "The rain?"

Lifting the cup the kid had brought him, the Damper poured liquid down his throat. Greasing the gears.

Here it comes, Tim thought.

The kid retreated to another table a good ten feet away, out in the middle of the room. One without even chairs, he had to go get one. He even brought one for his sister, which Tim suspected meant the Damper had gotten to him, too. Once his sister was there, though, he kept his eyes glued to the old man.

"You mean that screech? The one from a few minutes ago?"

Easing the Dark Mofo cap up his skull, the Damper revealed his single, protruding bat-ear. The one on the right. The left one wasn't there anymore. If the Damper had a story about where he'd lost that, he'd yet to tell it to Tim.

"Heard of the Dish?" he said.

From the tray table where she was still filling cups of soup, Mika laughed. Both kid and Damper ignored her. "What's the Dish?"

"Big satellite antenna," Tim said. "For listening to space."

The Damper tapped his one good ear. Possibly, he was grinning, now.

Even so, Tim found himself listening harder to the room. The barrage of banging overhead as rain pummeled the roof, which had all of them automatically raising their voices. He gazed around the bare, concrete walls. Loud as it had been, Tim was surprised the Damper *had* heard the screech. Caw. Whatever it was.

Mika appeared at his side, handed him a soup cup. "The Damper has mad skills," she said. It wasn't clear to whom.

The old man turned his leaky cat-eyes on her. Stared the grin off her face. "Like listening? Like respect for where you are? Like common sense?"

She opened her mouth, either to laugh or answer. Which is why, for one insane second, Tim thought the new shriek exploded from *her.*

Then they were all—the Damper, too—ducking, flinging glances up at the ceiling, around the walls as sound reverberated everywhere. Actually, it *wasn't* reverberating, Tim realized, there wasn't any echo in here, nothing to bounce off or from, so all this raging, blaring smoke-alarm shriek was *the sound itself*, happening now, which made it even crazier, drove all other thoughts but reaction out of his head except for the impossible idea that if anything, it was *louder* in here.

As if it were in here with them.

Then it wasn't. It also wasn't anywhere else. No echo or reverberation. No sound anywhere except rain.

"When you were out there today," the Damper said immediately, hand sliding off his ear to pull down his cap as he settled back in his chair. He grabbed up his coffee and blew on it. "Did you come across any tracks?"

Everybody else still had their hands near their heads, their shoulders hunched. It took them a few seconds to uncoil. To trust that the noise had shut off. Stopped.

Tracks? Tim thought, right as the dad said it.

"Tracks?"

"Railroad tracks."

Obviously. Tim shook his head at himself. "On the way to the cave," he said, then had to say it again to be heard. Mika was standing right next to him, but not leaning in. Not in their usual, comfortable way, even post break-up. He gulped some soup, which was miraculously hot, as always. Thick pumpkin taste coated his mouth. "Remember the signs?"

"Crossing Not in Use," the daughter said immediately.

"Observant one, you are," said Tim. "Good on you."

"Flirt," Mika murmured.

"Not those tracks," said the Damper, and just like that, he had them, the way he always did, sooner or later. There was nothing for it, even if they'd wanted there to be. Unfolding a chair, Tim started to offer it to Mika. But she'd already grabbed her own. They sat.

The Damper didn't look at any of them, but into the air over their heads. As though consulting winds. Conjuring not just memories or visions but the crystal ball to contain them.

Or else just scanning.

"The tracks I mean…these two, they know…" He waved a hand toward Tim and Mika. "These tracks haven't been in use for almost fifty years."

For a second, Tim wasn't sure he *did* know. Then Mika said, "Oh. Those." Quietly.

And Tim realized he did. He watched his former lover cradle her soup. If either of her hands had been free, he might have given it a squeeze. Which was probably why she kept them around the cup. So he addressed the Damper instead.

"We didn't get that far back. Or up. We're not totally insane. We didn't even need to, believe it or not, we actually saw—"

"So you're not complete drongos, then," said the Damper.

The family members, of course, were spellbound, in exactly the way they'd hoped to be when booking this day. All four of them watched the old man and said nothing.

"Laid more than a century ago, the tracks I have in mind." The Damper took a forkful of slice, shoveled it into his mouth. Went right on talking. "Narrow-gauge. For the gold rush, such as it was. There wasn't so much actual rush in this corner of Tassie. But then there was the logging. The mines that popped up, operating way back in those woods, up on those craggy hillsides. Not for long, not any of them. Not there."

Pausing abruptly, he aimed another long glance at the back wall of the Den. Eventually, he inclined his head as though genuflecting. Or acknowledging dominance. Both.

"Those places," he said. Slice crumbs flecked his lips and cheeks. "After a while. They…reject incursion. Hmm."

"Gilding the lily a bit, Damper," Tim muttered, meaning to tease, but even as he said it, he heard how he'd somehow fallen into rhythm. Filled his pre-ordained slot in the Damper's call-and-response spellcasting.

The old man mopped at his face with a napkin and somehow managed not to dislodge a single crumb. "Doesn't make it less true. It's a marvel, honestly—a testament—that those men even got those tracks laid. On inclines that steep." He made a near-ninety-degree slope with his hand. "Through rocks rooted in place, strangled in roots, immovable except when they all decide to move at once. Just drop down and obliterate everything. Not to mention the storms up there. The ones that seem to rise straight up out of the mountainside, like a tsunami of snow and ice, except sometimes the snow and ice aren't even *visible*. They're just on that wind. *In* that wind. They bury men right where they die, right there in the open. Killed by nothing. By nothingness. That's a real Tassie storm for you."

"Lily," Mika said. On her cue, Tim thought. He wondered if she realized it, too. "Gilding."

"And the *wildlife*," said the Damper, sliding suddenly forward, waving his hands and spreading them wide. "So much wildlife, we can't even imagine it, now. Or *you* can't. You have to have seen it."

"We saw all the roadkill," the mother said.

"I saw the most," said the daughter, and the Damper snorted.

"Roadkill. Now imagine before there was road, girl. Back then, in those woods, on those hills, at night, there was so much movement, it was like the planet was blowing bubbles. Wombats and kangaroos springing from a forest of their own shadows. Tree trunks crawling with so many snails and frogs and possums and squirrels that their bark seemed made of 'em. Everything, everywhere, jumping, foraging, *moving*. Fleeing."

"Fleeing what?" the father half-whispered.

The Damper spread his lips. Maybe he thought he was grinning. Teeth full of cake crumbs. What teeth there were. "Just so. Ask ten men who worked up there then—assuming you could find ten anymore, and assuming they'd talk to you—and you'd get ten different answers. I've heard people mention foxes fast as cheetahs, big as bears. Actual bears, as big as pine trees. I've heard wolves."

"Drop bears?" the kid piped up, and the Damper slammed that gaze down on him. Shut him up tight.

"But *officially*…" The old man waved a dismissive hand, not at the back wall this time, but toward the door. In the general direction, Tim knew, of Hobart, but also the rest of Australia. Civilization, period. "We don't have foxes here. Or wolves. Or bears." He did his spread-lips thing at the kid. "Drop or otherwise. Now, three of my grandfather's bunkmates, they came back from the woods one night swearing they'd seen a pack of thylacines tearing a screaming pademelon in half. Did you know pademelons can scream?"

After a few seconds, the mother whispered, "Which ones are the pademelons?"

"Like wallabies, Tim murmured, at the exact moment the daughter asked, "Is that what we heard?"

In response, Tim expected a full-force Damper glare. Instead, the old man laughed. At least, Tim had always assumed that was his laugh. Tonight, especially, it was closer to smoker's cough. Mostly scrape.

The son bobbed again on his seat. "Thylacine. Tasmanian tiger!"

"Just to be clear," said Mika, leaning back toward the wall, and for one startled, sweet moment, Tim thought she might do as she used to. Grab his hand with her warm, wet one and anchor him. "In the interests of science. The last thylacine died in a zoo on the mainland almost a hundred years ago."

"Herbert Murphy," said the Damper, turning his gaze on her, and whatever Mika was about to do with her hand, she stopped.

"What about him?"

"He had them on his cabin roof. Not five years ago. A month before he died." Into the Damper's mouth went a last shovelful of slice. The mouth chewed.

Bullshit, Mika didn't say.

So Tim said it for her. But the Damper ignored him. Ignored them all, really.

"Mostly, though, there were devils." Picking up his coffee, he held it to his mouth for a punctuation sip. But he never drank, didn't even blow, just left it there. He stayed that way a long time, staring at the back wall as though looking out a window, until the boy got restless. Or just excited.

"How many devils?"

"Oh," said the Damper. Steam rose from his cup, subtly distorting his face. The Den equivalent of a flashlight held under a chin. "So many, son. Like the bushes had mouths. Creatures would just fall into them, there'd be a clamor and snarling—you heard that snarl? Like a pig with a lion in its throat—and then that creature wouldn't be there anymore. Would be gone."

"Once again, for clarity," Tim said, "he means creatures that were already dead. Devils are scavengers, remember."

"Mostly," said the Damper.

Tim started to nod, caught a glimpse of Mika's face. Still weirdly hooded, frozen somewhere between smile and something very much else. The Damper noticed, too.

"Not that that was much comfort if you worked out there. Lived out there. To have your dog, say, just vanish one day, so completely that you never even found its bones…as if it had never been alive at all…They had to build fences to bury their dead. Otherwise, within days…" His fingers popped open. "Poof. Erased. That's the world we all decided we should strip. Plunder. And we succeeded. For a while. Those narrow-gauge tracks you didn't quite see? They're the fossilized remains of a whole human network. A monument to endeavor. For a few decades, we went up into those mountains and came down from the crags and ravines with logs, tin, zinc, silver, a little gold. It was like the whole region was a storehouse to raid. Ours for the taking. That's the world I grew up in. The cabin where I lived. People think of it as silent, now. Remote and barren as Mars. I still think of it as the loudest, most *living* place I've ever been.

"And then, the summer I turned eleven…"

Right in the pause, before the Damper said the words, Tim realized what the shriek—the one that triggered tonight's performance—really had sounded like. Sounded *exactly* like.

"That train," Mika said. As though reading his thoughts.

The Damper nodded. "The first one? The Wee Pandani? It was hardly even a train." Pushing his plate and cup away, he sat back, folded his arms. The movement looked mechanical and jerky, as though the guy was animatronic. "Those tracks. They could bear more than you think, but not much. Not what you have in your head as a freight train. Mostly, they were for getting crews and supplies up and down. Surprisingly sturdy, though. They'd been using that line since before the turn of the century. Through blizzards, Roaring Forties, hail so hard it punched holes in tin roofs. Up and down those slopes. There were stoppages every now and then, sure. A few derailments, nothing spectacular. Not one person dead, though. Not from the railways. Not one."

All four family members were leaning toward or into each other. The dad flashed a look at the mom. Amazed. Grateful. A family that understood their luck. The night they'd been gifted. Tim saw this, wished Mika would at least turn toward him. Then she did. Cup in hand, held at her waist. Face blank as the Damper's.

"Now, the Wee Pandani. It was just an engine and a passenger car. The passenger car empty, at least that night. Just an engineer and a stoker, making their way down to bring people back up. There was no storm. Bright moon. Nothing like this night."

"You tell it like you saw it," Mika snapped abruptly.

The comment seemed ridiculous to Tim, and also surprising. Of course the Damper told it that way. Secret of his magic.

So why accuse him of it now?

"No, no." The Damper didn't look at her. And yet, Tim had the uncanny sense that he was talking to her, alone. "No, I didn't see it. But the boys who did—out hunting late, when they shouldn't have been—they all told the same tale. Said they saw the Wee Pandini wind its way down the mountainside, as normal. Every now and then setting off its whistle, like it was waving."

Pursing his lips, taking a long, bumpy breath, the Damper unleashed a hoot. It came from the back of his throat, equal parts hum and hiss, as though he couldn't quite hold the tone or get it to catch.

Except that that was *exactly* what those trains sounded like. Tim had heard them in museums. Had even let Mika take him on one of those Christmas summer holiday excursions once.

The tourists had no basis for evaluation. But right as the Damper's sound gave way—seemingly melting into an echo that wasn't actually there, then splintering in the pounding rain—the father clapped. The mother, too.

The Damper didn't so much as lower his gaze. "The boys all said they saw the Pandani drop into those myrtle woods, nice and slow, just as it was meant to. Threading between the gorges and ravines the way it had a hundred times before.

"But it never came out. Never arrived in Hobart. Was never seen—by anyone—ever again."

As on so many other Damper nights, Tim felt simultaneous twinges of annoyance and comfort. This was the way the old man's stories always ended. Campfire-disappointing and strangely satisfying all at once.

Except tonight, the old man was still glaring right at him. As if this was less a tale than a prosecution.

"What?" Tim finally said.

"Did any of you even search?" Mika snapped. She, too, sounded angrier than the moment seemed to warrant.

Tim could almost hear those old lips stretch, like a seam popping open. "Search. Meaning what, exactly? Did we outfit mountaineering expeditions and rappel down cliff-faces, take our machetes, and hack to the bottom of those chasms—assuming they have bottoms—in the hopes of finding bodies? Wreckage? We did not. You want the cold, awful truth? What had we lost? Two cars. An engineer and a stoker. Tragic. Less loss than an average logging week in those woods, though, to be honest. At least in winter. In storm. Hardly worth the effort.

Again, the old man glanced toward the back wall. "Not like the second one."

Tim folded his arms across his chest, then felt ridiculous. What, exactly, did he need to defend? And from whom?

The Damper saw, though. Drilled those eyes into him.

"This was eleven years later. I wasn't even on the mountain by then. I was on the mainland. So all I know is what other people say they know. This train—the second—had a crew of miners on it, heading down for the summer holidays. Its engineer was old Levingston, the longest serving on all of Tassie. Half-aboriginal, with railroad ties for bones. Capable of blowing coal to life with his breath. So they say.

"That train was last heard just above Russell Gap, blowing whistles to the mid-morning sunlight and the wheeling birds. There's barely even a curve there. Plenty of gorges, mind. Rivers emptying down falls into pools so deep, no one's ever plumbed them, or bothered trying. Until then. So, theories abound. Anything *could* have happened. But if you're asking—and yes, young Daughter of the Hills, I see you are—what actually *did*...”

“Goddamnit,” Mika muttered, starting forward again as though she might...Tim didn't even know what. Throw coffee at the Damper? Burst out laughing, turn, and bow?

The parents shared another look. Gratitude. Self-congratulation. Amazement at being together backstage at the factory where memories get imprinted. Holding hands while rain drummed. If the shriek had gone off again, Tim would have been sure he really *was* in a play, or a dream. Something the Damper had magicked up, for his birthday party, maybe.

Except that now the Damper was glaring at Mika some more. “So you know. You knew it happened right around this time. You knew there was a storm coming. And yet, out you went.”

“Is that why they stopped using those tracks?” the son asked, oblivious.

Another few seconds passed before the Damper returned attention to him. “Oh no, son. That wasn't until the third one. The last one.”

“That's enough,” said Mika. So quietly that Tim was sure only he heard it. He stepped forward, touched her elbow, but she edged away.

Guilt whisked through him. About what, he had no idea. Regret, too. For this relationship that had almost worked. For this whole island world he'd decided on a whim to come to after uni, and discovered he loved. Even imagined himself part of.

Which seemed ridiculous, suddenly.

He watched the Damper. Ensconced in his chair, the old man seemed almost to emanate light, as though he were a projector. This whole place his movie. Shadows—or the ghosts of shadows, there being nothing in here actually to cast any—leapt around him. Ghost-wallabies of the air.

“This was long after most of the mines had closed. The logging camps packed up or just abandoned. The effort-to-yield ratio had grown too great decades before. So, no, son, none of this has anything to do with why those tracks stopped being used. It doesn't have anything to do with anything.

Except to the people who were on the train. And the people who still live here and care for their memory." Once again, the rheumy gaze swung to Mika. Taloned as a bird, threatening to sweep her away.

The Americans noticed nothing. They were too wrapped up in the story they were already telling themselves about the night they heard this story.

"Let's go," Tim whispered to Mika. "We don't have to stay. We've done our jobs."

"*You* go," she hissed back.

"Sightseers, this was," the Damper said. "Like yourselves."

Meaning not just the Americans, of course. Even Tim felt a *fuck you* bubbling up, and not just in Mika's defense. But saying it would have been like cursing a cliff or a fogbank.

"A holiday excursion train. One car. Mostly mainland tourists, but some so-called locals, too. Ho-Bart-ians. Out for a romantic weekend jaunt.

"This was so long after that second disappearance, almost no one even remembered it. Why would they? It had involved no one they knew. Twenty-six tourists. On a bright sunny day, at least down here. Up there…they say there were clouds, although I don't really know who 'they' are, since no one saw it happen. They say there might have been a freak mountain storm. One of the rare kind that boils up on those hillsides even in midsummer, like this one here tonight, except worse. Wind everywhere. Ice and snow flying around like the whole world is chipping apart.

"They made the top. Up above Russell gap. Afterward, a surveyor up there found a backpack one of the tourists had apparently forgotten, with a camera in it. Intact roll of pictures inside. All those happy people picnicking on the rocks, Whole families. Just like yours."

He grinned at the Americans. There was nothing kind in it, Tim knew. Nothing happy, or mean either. The facial-expression equivalent of wind.

"A carefree afternoon exploring old mining camps. Daring each other into the mouths of the mines themselves. Wandering in and out of abandoned sheds where actual people had lived.

As if this were all an attraction. Set up just for them. And *their* tour guides. Tasmania. All those animals. The trees. The gorges. The birds. But there's one shot. It's on the wall behind the circulation desk down in the Hobart Library, along with all those other historical snaps no one ever looks at. A group of twelve or so people, just about to reboard the train, in a sloping field of tall, wild grass. The sky stone blue, completely clear overhead. But on both sides, ringing the mountain, those black clouds. Whipping whorls of ice. As if they're all about to light out into the mouth of a wormhole. Trailing the thylacine into wherever it went. By steam gauge rail."

Once more, the Damper glanced toward Mika. Transfixed her. "Maybe you've seen such things," he said.

"Maybe I have," Mika answered. Her voice wavering. But not her answering glare.

"Hey," said the father, seemingly awakening from his trance, noting for the first time that there was some other story being told here. And it wasn't for them.

The Damper ignored him. Went right on. "Down they came. Into the maelstrom there must have been, given those clouds. Can you imagine? Actually, I think you can, given the night your intrepid guides chose to march you into. So there would have been wind sound. Maybe hail and rain, too. But also…"

Jerking with surprising speed to his feet, the Damper sucked in a deep, shuddering breath, rocking on his own legs like an engine clinging to tracks, and let loose.

He didn't quite get it right, Tim thought, even as he flung his hands over his ears. He couldn't come anywhere close to the volume, for one thing. But he *did* get overtones, somehow. Like one of those Tuvan throat singers. The top of his voice splitting into shriek, the bottom all but disappearing into his throat and out the bottom of his feet into the floor, where Tim almost believed he could feel it. Half earthquake, half roar. The whole family startled back, collapsing toward each other.

Only Mika didn't move. Stood there staring. Tears streaming down her cheeks, as irrelevant to her as rain to rock.

The Damper did it again. Better. Louder. Still not quite right. Definitely closer.

Then he fell back into his seat. Almost tipped off it, clutched the table, and sat there heaving like an old man.

Like the old man he was.

There was a long pause. Not nearly enough of one.

Then the kids burst out laughing. "You're so good!" the sister said.

"That's what you're saying we heard?" said her brother. "The last running of the great Tasmanian ghost train?"

At Tim's side, Mika leaned in again. Held on as the Damper gasped for breath, glanced at the back wall, the roof still thrumming and bucking as the rain hammered down.

"I thought you told me they showed you a devil," the old man finally said.

"They did!"

"And they told you how it eats?"

"Bones, claws," the boy chirped. "Keys. Cellphones. Everything."

One last time, the Damper smiled. Flat, ferocious smile. While the forest they'd fled barely two hours ago rose up in Tim's memory. Surged around him. Everything—devils, pademelons, wallabies, trees—up and roiling, raging. Running.

"No, son. Not the ghost of a train," the Damper said. "The ghost of what that train was running *from*."

Then he folded deep into his chair, crossing his arms over his chest. He closed his eyes as his Dark Mofo cap slid forward. The record player clicking off, Tim thought. Console shutting down.

Which should have been comforting. Would have been, if he could have gotten the woods out of his head. That primal, overwhelming need to *get clear* of them.

Overhead, rain drummed, though the wind had slackened. No more howling. Just drumming.

The father was the first to stand. He seemed to be fumbling with his smile, trying to get it to catch. One of the kids—Tim couldn't tell which—murmured, 'Thanks." Tim also wasn't sure whom the gratitude was for.

"Best walk them to their car," said the Damper, without opening his eyes.

But Tim was already up. Mika, too. Together, they shepherded their charges out of the Den and back down the breezeway to the parking lot. Free of that room, the old man's spell. The family was already chattering to each other. Laughing again. So they probably never even noticed Tim, then Mika, then both of them at once, glancing back at the hills they could no longer see. All those lives, animal and otherwise, marked and forgotten, predators and prey, tucked up for the night behind their curtain of rain.

PART TWO

…from the coasts…

Jetty Sara

Safe and warm inside the Brother J diner, hands around coffee mugs or tomato juices and mouths full of crab scramble, we watch the rain chase Li down the street. It's yipping at his heels, leaping on his back, and he's shuddering like a sheep hound by the time he flings open the door and staggers inside.

"Shut that, shut that!" Lulubelle shouts from her corner table, for form's sake since she's around behind the fireplace, and not one drop of wet is reaching her this morning. Dutifully, the rest of us take up the cry, and Li swings his head toward us, which sets a wave of water plunging off his hood down his face. He gives the whole room his snarl. Then he slams the door.

But he's Li, and by now he's grinning through his personal downpour. "How about we open the windows, get some air in?"

He takes one of the last available seats. It's too near the door, but most of us are already here, as usual when the storms roll in, so it's not likely he'll suffer much. His crab scramble and honey-toast side have beat him to his spot. He flops into his chair, does his sheep hound shiver, but he doesn't even get coffee in his mouth before Fresnel Tom snaps out of his slouch at the far end of the room as though someone has clicked him on. He stares back down the street the way Li came, toward all our tiny houses.

"Ah, shit," he says. "She's out."

All around the Brother J, forks fill with crab scramble, fly up towards faces. Cram in. We know what's coming.

"Who?" Li says, mid-chew. Again, for form's sake. Also because he just got here, wants at least to get warm.

"*God*damn," says Fresnel Tom.

"I thought she moved," Brother J calls from behind the counter. But he's coming out into the room, already heading toward the coat rack.

"Why would you think that?" Lulubelle snaps. "Only one way that *chica*'s leaving Swope City."

"The wet one," murmurs Old Ellis, and Lulubelle swats him hard as he stands.

"Shut up."

"You shut up," he snaps back. But he stands, too.

Then we're all at the window. The rain's crashing down so fat and hard, we don't see her at first (except Fresnel Tom, obviously, he's already seen her). It's also pre-dawn dark at eleven in the morning, so mostly what we see is our own faces. Cluster of fishermen and ex-fishermen and fishermen's widows and widowers, floating there in the glass as though underwater. That's not a thought any of us likes, not around here, and then Fresnel Tom points, and Old Ellis (who isn't older than the rest of us, just looks it) sighs.

"Shit. Yep."

She's so thin, even with that flappy black rain shell whipping around her, she looks like some sort of torn-loose sapling tumbling on the gusts. Except she's tumbling into them. Her hair is still the same color as that jacket, oil-slick black only without any swirls of color where light catches. Her skin—what we can see of it between spits of rain, flying hair—isn't exactly pallid, isn't any color, really. The color of sidewalk. A surface you walk on.

"*Pobre chica*," Lulubelle murmurs.

"Pathetic bitch," says Li. Even though it's his fault she's out there. He's the one who told her the story.

No one swats him. No one argues. Twelve years since the sea did this whole town a solid, sucked her John and his whole monstrous crew off our streets and out of our lives, but everyone here still has memories. Probably, everyone has some they haven't even shared.

"Well, come on," says Brother J, flipping up his hood.

"You come on," says Old Ellis. Again, for form's sake. He's already zipping in. We all are.

We wait a few seconds longer, until she's well past, halfway down the hill to the beach. Not that she'll see us or care if she does. *Pobre chica* on a mission, that's our Sara. Li's coat is still dripping so hard, it's like he's got a personal rainstorm right on top of him. It makes Fresnel Tom and Lulubelle laugh.

"Hilarious," says Li. He pulls the door open, and we're out in it.

The downpour has actually slackened some, but the wind's up, and it shoves against us as we trail along toward the water. Reminds us of those days—that one horrible year—when they were among us, John and his crew. The shoves when they passed us constant, casual, like we were doors to throw open, cats to kick. Not people at all. Sources, at best, of supplies they might need. Of sons they could hook on whatever cut product they'd scored and couldn't offload in Eureka or Medford. Daughters to rape.

"*Yo-ho*," one of us, probably Old Ellis, murmurs, and the shudder whips through our whole group.

If it's a pirate's life for you, you better be goddamn sure you're a pirate.

"Look at her," says Li. He sounds regretful, apologetic, which is ridiculous. No one blames him. He was trying to help, same as we all have at one point or other. "Straight for the goddamn jetty."

That's where she's headed, all right. Across the beach, feet catching in stands of washed-up kelp and trailing them behind her, which makes her look like some skeletal black fish wriggling free of a net. Her hair whips and flaps.

"Move it," says Lulubelle, but we're already picking up the pace. From the top of the hill at the edge of town, all you can see is harbor, but even that's shuddering today, the boats tilting and turning on their tie-ropes, banging against their births or the dock like bells being rung.

Of course, you can barely hear them over the ocean. Halfway down the hill we see the sea, and then we move even faster.

"*Come back, Sara!*" Li bellows abruptly, his voice boomeranging right around in his face. There's no way she could hear him, not over all that roaring and smacking and splashing. Even if she could, there's no way she would listen.

By the time we've hit the beach, she's up on the jetty, head down, marching straight through that gauntlet of state-generated WARNING: TSUNAMI ZONE signs, then the homemade ones we put up, partly for tourists, mostly for her. The one with the stick figures tumbling into heaving abyss over the words TSUNAMIS. SERIOUSLY. The one we had painted right onto metal of the wreckage of this harbor in January of '64.

Surprisingly, just as we reach the edge of the water and take up post in the lee of our ridiculous Swope City Light, Sara half-turns our way. We get a good look at her sidewalk-skin face. With a jolt that hits us all together—a wave crashing in—we remember what she looked like, then. Right before John and his crew came. While they were there, too, if we're honest. Just as thin. But majestic, somehow. Grown into herself, lean and wild.

She's gone all beaky, now, like some wounded sea bird abandoned by the flock. Skimming the beach to scavenge leavings.

She isn't looking at or responding to us, needless to say. She's seen something in the water. Thinks she has. Stops a second, starts to crouch.

"Ah, fuck," says Fresnel Tom.

Old Ellis shivers. Then we're all doing it. We watch, shivering, until she straightens. For one magical second, she looks like she's coming back this way. Then she glances up into the rain, raises both arms, and flips us the bird.

Birds.

Spinning away, she launches again down that spit of rock and pavement. Our imaginary divide between Swope City and open ocean, that we still catch ourselves imagining keeps us safe. Time after time, in spite of everything.

Spray flies up around her with every step, as though she's causing it. Like a little girl, puddle jumping. Pretty soon, from where we stand, it's hard to see jetty at all. She looks like she's walking on water. Hiking straight out to sea.

We're not close enough, now, and we know it. If the worst comes—wave, sure, but more likely, her deciding just to go ahead and jump, fling herself into the arms of the man she seems utterly sure is waiting for her just below the surface—we'll never reach her in time. We should go out there with her. At least a few of us are pretty clearly going to have to, today.

At least the rain has thinned. Even the wind is sputtering, spitting gusts but no longer hurling itself in our faces. The ocean's still slamming around out there, but it's gone a lighter gray, looks more like it does when it lets people near or on it. Frisky, like.

"I'll go," says Brother J.

"Me, too," says Li. But neither of them move yet. Sara's stayed standing instead of kneeling out there on her jetty, and she's not moving much. Again, there's something birdlike about her. Like a hovering gull, holding its place in the currents of air.

"Oh, Goddamn it," says Fresnel Tom, but not about Sara, and he steps off the sand to the side of the jetty and splashes through the shore water toward the Lighthouse.

We call it a lighthouse. I guess it is. It's still hard to believe it ever really worked. It's tall enough, I suppose, a good 20 feet high, and it has withstood more than its share of weather. But the land it is slowly sinking into was never a raised point, is blocked from sight of most open water by the curve of the coast, and isn't even accessible when the tide's up and the water completely covers the narrow, sandy spit connecting it to the beach. Tom's been working on it for years, scraping decades-deep coatings of bird shit off the sides and getting new glass made for the windows and seeing to the machinery. Even so, it looks mostly like a model lighthouse that washed up here from somewhere. Cracked concrete, a rusted metal door that Tom keeps boring new bolts into, and which the ocean keeps pushing open and rushing through. Leaning Tower of Lighthouse.

Reaching the door, Tom stares down at the water gushing over his feet and inside, laying on yet another layer of damp upon damp. He bangs the door with his fist, and it rings.

"Oh, hon," says Lulubelle. Not about Tom, we know, and we all swing together, again, toward the jetty.

Sara's still not kneeling. Not yet. But she's all leaned over, staring down as the splash hurls itself up the stones, over her boots. She has her hands out straight, and her mouth has started moving. If you didn't know better, had never stood near enough when she gets like this, you could mistake what she's doing for conjuring. What she's really up to is worse, of course. Breaks your heart, every time.

She's cooing.

Brother J makes a clucking noise. Part sympathy, part disbelief. "It's like she really believes it, you know?"

"It's not *like* that at all," murmurs Li. Then says it again, louder, because it's hard to make him out over the whapping water, and he wants us to hear his regret. "She *does*."

Right on cue, down she drops. Her hands, at least for now, are back in the pockets of her windbreaker, but they won't stay there. She's not leaning yet, anyway. Then she is.

There's no way we can see her face. Too much spray flying around, like the world's being painted into being—or chipped *out* of being—right in front of us. But every single one of us knows she's smiling.

It's our oldest city tale, the one we've all not just heard but told. Practically our motto. In high summer, on the right night, with the Brother J humming and the midnight crab-scrambles flying, some caught-up tourist or other will ask the right question of the right person, and just like that, we'll be reciting. Faces in the waves. The way, in storms, the water sometimes gives you glimpses of people it has taken from you. Their visages so solid, so precisely as you best remember them, that you expect them to open their watery mouths and gurgle hello. This is what passes, when you live by the grace of the ocean, for mercy.

On the jetty, amid the rioting spray, our Sara stretches out her hands.

It's not raining anymore. For whatever difference that makes. There's so much wet flying around in the air, it's a wonder we can breathe it. Another old Swope City tale. Half-gilled, we are.

"Like she's begging him to take her," Lulubelle murmurs, something very near a catch in her voice. Or else simple wind-borne wetness. We're watching hard, now. When she leans forward even a little more—which she will, any second—we're going to have to move. Make sure we're closer.

"If it were really him," says Old Ellis, "he fucking would. Not for love. For sheer meanness."

"If it were him," says Brother J, "he wouldn't stop at her."

For no reason we can see, Sara glances back in our direction. Stares hard. Seems to, anyway. We all feel it.

"Maybe she's telling him to go ahead."

It takes longer than usual, today. She's got her hands out, and we're pretty sure her mouth's still moving. But she's just crouched there, and the spray riots around her for so long that she almost melts into the landscape. Jetty, leaning lighthouse, ship-masts in the harbor, cloud mass, darker cloud mass. And our Sara. Beacon, buoy. Something on which to focus, so you can watch the world roll.

Every single one of us—Tom, too, from up in his beloved light—is watching. Looking right at her. Mesmerized, in the way looking at that ocean does that to you. A miraculous, cleansing sensation on the right day. Transcendental. A reason to stay.

And yet, somehow, not a single one of us sees. How is that possible?

We see *her,* okay. Don't process, but we all see. Her *reared back,* not leaning forward. Arms straight out in front, palms forward. Not defensive, but not reaching, either. Words fly from her mouth like whitewater. Hang in the air.

It should be terrifying. The fact that we can hear her.

We've had it wrong, we all think together, as one thought, one thing thinking, not a bunch of town nobodies living our separate grieving, peaceful, nobody lives.

Then Li says, "Oh."

Even then, it takes us a second we do not have to understand. To make sense of the fact that we aren't collectively imagining what our Sara is saying, but really hearing it. Because the wind hasn't just dwindled; it has dropped off the face of the world. The sea hasn't just ceased slapping and slamming but vanished. Literally *is not there*. The boats in the harbor clunk as they drop down on rocks and sand that moments ago were bottom. The jetty looms, suddenly towering, like the top of a just-risen island, brand new and streaming. There's a moment of blissful silence like no one in Swope City has experienced, ever, during one second of our lives on this Earth.

Finally, one of us screams, *"Run!"* Not just at Sara but all of us. By this point, we're already running. Obviously. As if running could make any possible difference now.

At some level, we really are one entity, at least in this instant. No one makes any decision. Certainly, no one calls out commands. But there we all are, lunging instinctively across the exposed sand toward the lighthouse. Tom is up top, watching us, not the sea—the not-sea, absence of sea—and screaming. We're all screaming, just not words.

Except Sara. She's screaming words.

The silence gets swallowed. That's the best I can do to describe it. It doesn't erupt or shatter. It's simply subsumed. As we tumble, screaming, through the lighthouse door, swing together to paw and shove at it in a desperate attempt to get it shut (as if shutting that door is going to matter), Lulubelle stops just long enough to glance outward. To see.

"So many faces," she whispers. Except she can't possibly be whispering, because we couldn't possibly hear her.

The rest of us never see. We just somehow sense it roaring in. Less trampling the word than rolling it up, sucking it into itself. It's not a wave, that's a ridiculous word for it. It's not a wall, either. It's the world folding over, slamming itself shut. Some of us are up the stairs with Tom, some of us still on the stairs when it hits.

After that, for who knows how long—probably not very long, not in time as we have charted it up until then, before realizing that time is as fragile and mutable and imaginary as everything else we have ever collectively decided equals *living*—there is no sound but roar. No thought, no sensation, not even panic. We are all tumbled together, twisted around each other, but we're not even aware of our own bones and bodies, let alone anyone else's. Not only are there no words, there's no reason for words. Nothing to communicate.

Just nothing.

From outside, Old Ellis will say later, it must have looked almost funny. Miraculous, sure, but also ridiculous. Almost as absurd as being awake and alive at all.

Somehow, our lighthouse keels slowly, slowly, all the way over. Like a giant's hand lowering us to the ground. Leaving us lying there twisted together, soaked and floating, banged and bruised. Barely really rumpled at all. It takes a while to figure out which way is up—meaning out—and then disentangle, crawl toward the gaping spaces where the lens windows had been and into the open air and reeking wet. Which is already receding.

The Swope City Miracle. None of us named it that in the moment. Somehow, that was already what this was. The biggest tsunami ever to hit this coast. Pouring all the way up our hill and out the other side of town. Flooding buildings, knocking down road signs.

Killing no one. Not one person.

Except Sara. Obviously.

Every single night we gather at the Brother J, since then—among tourists, all together, alone, whatever—we raise our tomato juices to her. We're not exactly toasting. Not apologizing. Not even memorializing. Just acknowledging.

We've never talked about what we saw, what we heard. There's no need. We've figured it out on our own. Sara on her knees on her jetty. Her hands outstretched like that. Not as though reaching for her lover. More soothing a big cat. Stroking its humped up fur.

Telling it no. No, babe, no.

Let them go.

Slough

"Wait 'til you hear why," I said into my phone. I had it wedged between my shoulder and ear so I could repack my cameras.

"Why?" said Daniel in that tone he's perfected: interested in spite of himself. It's partly an act, he knows I know it, and it doesn't matter; it's sexy to me.

"The rain."

"What?" The laugh is not an act, and the actual key to the sexiness. Daniel is interested. It's the in-spite-of he plays at.

"You heard me. Actually, not the rain. The storm."

"It's storming?"

"Did I say it was storming?"

"Gabby, just—"

"Don't you read the weather? There could be thunder. This is a family organization, remember."

"Oh god, that's so good. All white supremacists must wait at least thirty minutes after lightning strikes before re-donning jackboots."

I set down my bag and leaned against the bridge railing, watching the gray-green, relocated Woonasquatucket pool docilely below. The bridges didn't really make Providence look like Venice, I decided. But they heightened my awareness of the decay I could almost smell beneath all these swanky, restored facades, or lurking just out of sight down the surrounding blocks.

That block, there, say, past the First Baptist Church in America, where Roger Williams set up shop after the Puritans kicked him out for learning Native languages and railing against slavery.

Ironies.

"Ooh, but I forgot. The trip wasn't a total waste. Daniel…they've found a third F."

"A…okay, what?"

"…of the Fox, Daniel. They're now the Faith Families of the Fox. They have a banner. It has a fox on it."

"You're fucking kidding."

"They should add Fervent. Then they would have four Fs."

"Yeah, and then they'd be…medically excused?"

"Hah." I was laughing for real, though. Daniel, too. Sometimes, we really do feel like lovers. Talk like lovers. Usually not when we're trying to be lovers, though. Overhead, clouds scudded, gray and grimy, like smokestack smoke but pumped from up there, in some decrepit factory of the air.

I didn't want to go back to the Bronx yet. Not to the tiny basement office from which Daniel and I ran the photos-for-commercial-reuse business we'd kept solvent for more than seven years. Not to Daniel's nearby one-room, half-bath apartment we sometimes shared. Certainly not to the Staten Island studio efficiency I'd inherited from a wastrel uncle, paid rent control for, and had last seen weeks ago because it just took too long to get there. Right then, none of those places felt like mine. I wondered when I'd last had a place that felt like mine. College, maybe. At the school I'd named NW NoPlace.

But that wasn't the moment I decided to call Julian. Why would I even have thought of him then?

"Did you get a shot of her at least? Gab?"

I hate Gab. He knows it. Maybe he sensed I wasn't coming back and was annoyed.

"Of Mrs.—sorry, Dr. Tilley? I did indeed. That hair, Daniel. It's huge. It really is like waterfall spray. You've never seen old lady hair that wild. She stood on this bridge like Grandma Moses—"

"Probably not so much like Grandma Moses. Who didn't have wild hair, I don't think."

"More like her than you'd think. More than you'd want to believe. Okay, Dr. Tilley has more hair. But she's little, full of sparkle, big violet eyes, keeps a pug-nosed, pasty grandkid on each arm. 'We are not like the fox that roams these hills,' she said. Have you heard her speak? There's nothing little about that voice. Like a fucking hanging judge. 'We are not like the fox. We are the fox.'"

"Just one?" Daniel laughed again.

"'For this land and of it. It is us. We are it.' The woman is magnetic, Daniel. Scary as shit."

He heard the anxiousness in my voice, or disgust, or whatever it was. He stopped laughing but too late.

"I'm staying here today. I need to... I'll be home tomorrow."

Some, rare times—when I'm tired, drinking, aware of being 38 and still not sure I actually don't want children, or when I decide out of nowhere I'm not coming back and he doesn't protest—I still think I could marry Daniel. If he still wants me to or ever really did.

Bugs clouded the surface of the water, hummed in the grass at either end of the bridge. But none came for me. The sticky morning heat slicked my skin but hadn't suffocated me. The protesters and counter-protesters, such as they had been, had dispersed, and hours would pass before business lunchers streamed into the park. Dr. Tilley had called for bonfires all along the redirected bank, fox flags and white pride in the streets, smoke in the air. Even without all of that, Providence felt far from the city or country I imagined I lived in. Which consisted mostly, honestly, of New York now.

"The FFF," Daniel murmured.

"Got it in one, as our former overlords across the pond put it."

"But... Ku Klux Klan. Isn't that supposed to be the sound of a rifle being cocked? What's FFF, then?"

"A fart when it's tired?"

We both laughed.

"You sure you don't want to come home, Gabby?"

That was what actually caused it: the word home in my ear in his voice, at once overfamiliar and detached. A euphemism. In the weirdly airless gusts of breeze, the gaps of gray between grayer clouds massing, on the matte-flat surface of water that reflected nothing, certainly not me, I could feel—could actually see—myself floating. Drifting in that liminal space between lives where most people I know live.

Julian lives here, I suddenly remembered. In Rhode Island, somewhere.

"See you tomorrow, Daniel," I said, disconnected from him, and swiped to my contact screen.

Even there, Julian showed up out of order and adrift, the only person filed by nickname: Boom. I had no idea if the number was current. For an address, what I had was SOUTH COUNTY? I'd added his wife's name, but apparently hadn't been sure of that either, because LORI had a question mark, too. When had I last even heard from him?

In R.I., I texted, heart hammering for no good reason. R u?

His answer pinged before I got my phone back in my pocket.

COME. Please?

Not "Hi." Not "Who is this?" or "Gabby. Wow."

COME. Please?

It was an archetypal electronic communication, so denuded of meaning that it could have meant anything I feared or wanted. I've learned the dangers of interpreting texts like that the same painful way most people do.

But Julian apparently wanted me to come to wherever he was. Really did. How often does that happen with other adults, if we're honest? An invitation without any suggestion of whatever they're swamped with and will have to put aside, audible grinding of gears as days get recalibrated and to-do lists assessed, hesitation over the room that's thank god clean-ish or isn't? How much more peaceful and comfortable our friends look in the glowing little fish-tanks of our phones. They hardly even need feeding.

Come where? I responded.

Within an hour, I was headed south down the 1A in a tiny rented Civic. The tininess proved crucial, as I almost grazed three parked cars maneuvering free of the jammed lot onto a packed downtown street better suited to bike messengers than drivers. Admittedly, the problem might have been that I hadn't driven in five years.

Once out of the city, the road opened up. Traffic didn't exactly evaporate, but it loosened, chaperoning me down-country, over bridges, past bays glimpsed through trees. So many trees. Maples, oaks, American beach, all bursting with bright summer green under threatening gray sky. I passed signs for harbors, bridges, a lighthouse, a pond. How small does your state have to be before you start signing ponds? Every now and then, I'd get a glimpse of gray water, red brick buildings huddled on some hilltop rise, picnic tables in clearings. Mostly, though, the trees hemmed me in, decorous and stately and weirdly intimidating as Buckingham Palace guards. Welcome to look, I imagined them saying, in some invented accent that was probably more Down East—not even the right state—than Rhode Island. Beautiful, yes? Keep moving.

Once, trapped behind a seafood truck with painted crabs scuttling over it, and with rain clouds still blanketing the landscape, I glanced left and thought I saw faces in the branches of a maple across the freeway. Pasty, grinning, long-nosed. Dr. Tilley's grandkids in their centuries-old tree-blinds. Fox-kids who could climb. To absolutely no one, and for reasons having mostly to do with being afloat in a day I hadn't planned, I waved. The faces dissolved into the branches and leaves and the patches of blank sky between them.

The drive took longer than it should have. Rhode Island is forty-some miles long, and traffic stayed light. The freeway, such as it was, ended but the road kept going. There were turnoffs for the 1, the 2. Directional signs for Jamestown. Jerusalem. Trees got scruffier, hunkered back. Towns appeared: low clapboard gas stations, red-cedar main streets with taverns at one end and ice cream shops at the other. Still, Julian-land did not appear.

Finally, having caught red at all three stoplights in a town comprised of a Check Cashing Laundromat, a hardware store, and an incongruous Luxury

Living Real Estate office, I pulled into a sandy parking lot. There was ocean ahead, now, or water, anyway. It seemed I was pointed straight off the end of the island.

I'd taken the place I stopped for a gas station, possibly abandoned. But when I got out of the car, I heard voices pouring through the screen door of the squat, square hut at the back of the lot. "Shut up, Cindy," some kid said. Then came a clank, a mechanical gurgle, some sloshing. Slushie or Soft-serv sounds, from faltering machines.

Like coming home, I thought, though nothing about that made sense. I hadn't been "home", meaning Iowa, since my mom died, and Slushie sounds gurgled somewhere in the strip-malls around every American's "home", and I'd never been to Rhode Island in my life.

Think I missed you, I thumbed into my phone. Pretty sure that last sign said South Carolina.

Julian's answer, again, came back instantaneously.

Keep going.

Don't you want to ask where I am? I threw in a smiley-face emoji for good measure. I do that when I'm unsure of myself. Julian, I remembered, had always made me feel this way, which was kind of funny, given Julian.

I stood there a long time but got no additional response.

The restaurant—quick-stop, lemonade stand, whatever—did have a sign, I saw now. It was hand-painted, leaning out of the dirt by the screen door, staked like a tomato plant to keep it upright. But instead of a name, the sign boasted two declarations, both hand-inked: WHERE TUNA COMES TO LIFE, and under that, SMALL STATE. BIG FLAVOR.

Reaching back into the Civic, I grabbed a camera, headed inside. There were only three people in there, two freckle-faced brothers and Cindy, I presumed. Cindy was taller than either boy, spindle-armed, long-legged, pointy as a shark fin. None of them looked older than sixteen. I snapped some shots before they even processed my entrance: three kids; serving counter full of cardboard vats behind cooled glass that should have held ice cream but instead contained tuna salad variants; chopping counter, scratched-all-over silver, shiny-clean.

"Ok, kids," I said. "Bring tuna to life."

Which, I had to admit, back in my car and another twenty minutes down the endless spit between bays and tiny towns, they absolutely had. It wasn't even whatever they'd spiced it with, which wasn't much, honestly. It was the freshness, still tingling on my lips, my tongue, way down my throat. So fresh I half-thought I could feel it flipping around, reconstituting. A bracing taste, not entirely pleasant.

"New York?" Cindy had asked, dead flat, folding my sandwich perfectly into its wrapper.

Iowa, I'd wanted to say and almost did. Why? As an expression of solidarity? I'm you, not me? For you and of you? I'd snapped her picture again and offered to send it to her. She'd just shrugged.

I still wonder how long that drive actually lasted. There's only one road, and it's the one I drove. But I'm convinced that if I ever went back, took Daniel—I've considered it, he's asked—that road would empty into water a good hour before we actually got to Slough. We'd maybe see Slough floating on the horizon, a place the country once connected to. But we wouldn't be able to drive or walk there.

The first, fat raindrops spattered on my roof and hood, as though a horse had galloped past overhead. One if by land, I remember thinking. Humming, even. To my right, inland, a curve of water lay tucked into the land, serene and waveless. The scatter of moored sailboats there twitched in the spits of drizzle like the ears of sleeping cats. To my left, down weed-pocked streets, the ocean roiled.

Boom, I thought, and with a surprised snort, remembered why we'd called Julian that. All this time, I thought I'd coined it, a trademark Gabbyism referring ironically to his elusiveness, his ability to be in a room without so much as rippling the air let alone tilting a conversation, unless he was playing guitar. But that wasn't it at all.

All through our heads-down, two-jobs-plus-classes, finish-fast-before-the-money's gone lives at NW NoPlace—a particularly rank Gabby-ism for our not-little, undistinguished Midwest university, our Directional School for those without direction planted squat in the middle of a dying college town (meaning a dead town with a college in it), somewhere I'd actually genuinely loved and still missed—Julian kept disappearing. Sometimes he'd do it right in the middle of a term, sometimes two days into one. He'd be gone two weeks, a month. The last time, he stayed away three years, and Daniel and I had long since decamped for my inherited Staten Island studio by the time he returned. He never said where he went, not even when he came back. But he always wrote from his home—from Slough—right before he reappeared.

Daniel had given him the name, not me. Boom, as in boomerang.

There weren't many signs of any kind along my road by that point. Certainly none that said SLOUGH 4 mi. or anything. All drive long, the clouds had been congealing into a single, miles-long, fathoms-deep thunderhead. But now, when I stopped staring around for markers long enough to glance up, I saw only wispy gray which was no longer congealing or even moving. The rain thinned and steadied. Instead of beating, it beaded on my windshield and hood, draping me in itself. It was like going through the world's longest mechanical car wash, except instead of scrubbing off road-grit, it was coating me in it.

Then I was there. I'm not even sure how I realized it; there was no fancy Narragansett Towers landmark, no banner announcing an upcoming Crafts and Crabs Fair. I know I saw the words SLOUGH LIBERTY-GUARDIAN on a dirt-caked newspaper box, the kind you put a quarter in and then pray the lid actually lifts so you can get your paper out. The words were white, fading into metal which was rusted, pocked with holes.

There wasn't a curb. The street, which I guess counted as paved—more sprinkled with paving crumbles, but there was paving involved—seemed to pool between buildings, flowing like shore water up to and underneath the weedy grass and dirt paths that abutted the scatter of storefronts. Most of the structures were clapboard, single-storied, the windows filthy. Along the bases, especially, the remaining paint was coated in a yellow-brown rime which could have been street-muck or salt decay or markings from the coyote packs I suddenly imagined roaming this street after dark. Assuming there were coyotes in Rhode Island.

Mostly, Slough looked past its use, the buildings soft, somehow, permeable, vulnerable, like covered wagons ossified in place. Feeling sneaky even with no one around, I rolled down my window and snapped surreptitious photos. Then I grabbed my phone off the passenger seat.

The first thing I typed was Wow. Can see why you always came back. Then, annoyed with myself, I deleted that and just asked for directions.

Those proved surprisingly elaborate, and ended with When in doubt, go left.

I went left. Paving crumbled away, became dirt or maybe sand. It didn't so much grind under my wheels as suck at them. Trees sprang up on either side of the road, all different kinds. Oaks, beeches, elms, maples, a cherry or two, broken-branched or stripped of bark all the way up their trunks or just pocked and pecked all over. They were all still alive, though. It was like driving through some pre- or maybe post-industrial trainyard, but for decommissioned trees instead of engines.

Between trees, set back from the road on irregular lots, I glimpsed houses with fences, some two-story, some ranch, clapboard or stone, hunkered against the rain. Once—and only once—I caught sight of two kids way back in a marshy clearing with a couple tipped-over bikes in the long grass between them. As I watched—but not because they noticed me watching—they launched into side-by-side sprints and then threw themselves into the reeds, which swallowed them.

Like eagles after shrews, I thought as I drove, bore left some more, wondering how much more left there could possibly be.

Or kids with a Slip-n-Slide. I smirked at myself in the rearview mirror.

One more left, and suddenly I was back on pavement, gliding down some sort of frontage road between, on one side, slumped houses with leaning verandas and neatly mowed lawns, and on the other sand dunes. Every now and then, the dunes dropped and paths opened between them. Down those paths, I saw ocean, gray in the drizzle.

The strangest thing about those houses was the way they angled into their lots, turned at least partway toward each other instead of the street. Settle onto those tilting porch-swings or cheap wicker chairs, and you'd be staring not at passing cars or the dunes but into your neighbors' front windows. Again, I thought of frontier wagons circled for safety or company or both. The street ended in a cul-de-sac, and on the veranda of the white two-story at the very back of that—just maybe the literal last house on land—I spotted Julian with his guitar.

His guitar!

I hadn't thought about that in so long. To call Julian's flamenco playing his trademark at NW NoPlace would have been overstating. Vanishing was his trademark. But a couple times a quarter, he got on the bill at the folk pub under the dining hall and did a set that wowed the thirty or so of us in attendance, if only because it seemed so out of place and character, for him, the school, the whole state. The country as we knew it. Stocky, paste-skinned, flop-blonde Julian in his New England Patriots hat, strum-stuttering through Spanish rhythms as though born to them.

Was he even good, I wondered now as I rolled gently to a stop in the curve of the cul-de-sac? Rain ticked over the roof and windshield, blearing the lawn. Stepping out, I expected breeze but felt none. In the open air, the rain made almost no sound at all, barely even moved the leaves on the trees. Julian raised a hand with a pick in it and waved. Then he stutter-strummed. It was impossible not to move across the grass to that rhythm. So I did that, shyly. I swayed a bit, dragged a foot, then flung it in front of me. Julian smiled and kept playing.

One thing I knew: he'd seemed awfully good at 12:30 on a Saturday night in the pub under NW NoPlace. He sounded good still.

He'd balded on top since I'd seen him last, the hair just as messy but sparser, like beach grass. His cheeks had maybe spread a bit, but he'd always had wide cheeks, a little snowman's nose, flat blue eyes that got bluer toward the center, as though whatever was behind them dropped off at the pupil, got deeper. He had one of those not quite definable faces, handsome when you thought about it except you wouldn't. Didn't. It was a running joke with Daniel and me, had stayed one all these years. We'd see an actor in some movie or show, and one of us would say, "Hey. He looks like Julian." It was always true. The joke was that none of those actors looked like each other.

"Hi!" he said, smiling wide, then blushing. "Gabby. You're here."

"Hey, Boom." I would have hugged him except for the guitar. "What's it been, fifteen years?"

He turned toward the screen door of his house. "Girls, hurry up," he called. "Don't forget towels."

I'd heard he was a parent, probably from him. Years ago. But watching him be one caused a twinge of ache or else just surprise. As in college, Julian wore a faded, no-color t-shirt at least three sizes too big that draped him like a little kid's cape, and yet I got the sense that he'd taken on weight. His exact shape seemed even harder to define than I remembered.

"Hmm," he said. "You look…"

I caught myself leaning in, weirdly anxious. Busy? Older? Energized? Harder? All things I knew I was. Feared I was. Celebrated about myself.

But this was Boom, practical in his human interactions if nowhere else in his life. "…Yep. I think one of one Lori's would fit you. Want to swim?"

From inside, I heard clattering, scrambling. A girl's shriek, then laughter. The pop of plastic food container lids pried open or snapped shut. Kitchen drawers rattling open. Already, before he confirmed it—did he ever actually do that?—I knew this was the same house Julian had always vanished to.

Glancing over my shoulder, I remembered the rain. "Swim? At a pool?"

"In the ocean."

"It's…" Even as I said it, I felt the absurdity. Looking back now, from the Bronx, and my life, and land that's actually on land attached to the world, I know what I meant. But at the time, I felt ridiculous. "…wet," I finished anyway.

Julian raised an eyebrow. Then he said, "I'm so happy you're here. You have no idea." He rolled a Spanish chord before opening the screen and leaning the guitar against a wall inside. "Come in."

I was moving through the door he held open as I asked, "What if Lori wants to swim?" So I didn't actually see him flinch. It's possible that the pause I remember is one I inserted.

"Lori's…" Instead of finishing, he gave a wave of his hand in the direction of the yard, the rain, the road. He could have meant she was at the cleaners or visiting her mother or doing Tae Kwan Do for all I know. He didn't, though.

She was gone. Whether that meant dead or just away from Julian, I wasn't sure then and am not now.

The whole house ticked. I only saw the one grandfather clock opposite the front entryway, wedged under the staircase. It must have been gorgeous once, a century old at least, the finish on the beechwood casing glossless now, faded and speckled all over with what could have been bug smear, salt decay from the air, or even sand, the wood itself not so much warped as softened, sickly looking, like liver-spotted skin, the panes of glass across the face and workings bleared by layers of fingerprints that had been wiped at but not away. Despite its condition, that clock didn't so much tick as thump, steady and fierce as a heartbeat.

There had to have been more clocks, though. Ticking and tick-echoes poured from overhead and through the walls on either side of the surprisingly close, low-ceilinged entryway. I felt it through my shoes, in the floor.

"Doesn't it bother you?" I asked Julian's back as he hurried down the hall into a bedroom. Air moved the moisture on my bare arms. In the breaths between ticks, I thought I heard a fan somewhere. Fans.

Because of the rain, I was having trouble processing how hot it was. Smothering, midsummer-Atlantic Coast awful. In the kitchen, giggling erupted like birdsong. Instinctively, my lips pursed to shush it, but I stopped myself. Why did that sound seem too loud for the house, which already shuddered all over with sounds? And who was I to decide?

Julian reappeared with towel and bathing suit draped over his arm, saying, "Doesn't what?"

If I tried, I don't think I could design a one-piece black bathing suit as ugly as the one he handed me. I can't even tell you what made it so hideous, or how I could tell even before he held it out. The blackness had leached from the lycra, for one thing, leaving a sort of husk-black, like sun-bleached beetle shell. The straps were bulky, blocky, like links of chain.

It felt like a bathing suit, though. Idiotically, what passed through my head was, It'll keep off the rain.

"The ticking," I said. "I mean, it's amazing, but how do you sleep?"

Julian glanced past me toward the kitchen. "Girls," he said.

Meaning, shush? Or, Come meet the guest? The word had no impact as far as I could see.

He grinned again. "Inherited. The clocks. Family heirlooms. One of my great-great-greats made them, I think. Or, um." He stopped grinning, watched me, gave a little shrug. "I mean, his slaves did. On my mom's side."

"Slaves? In Rhode Island?"

"Biggest percentage of any northern colony."

Somehow, that information just made the sounds more insistent. "And… you sleep to this? This doesn't bother you?"

"Only when one's out of step."

My knees twitched just at the thought. "Oh my God. That would drive me screaming batshit. Wait. Boom, when that happens, how do you go about—"

"Don't you live in the Bronx?"

"The Bronx doesn't tick."

"It makes every other sound known to mankind, pretty much all the time. Right? Are those sounds ever in unison or alignment?"

Again—from here and now—those questions only tangentially relate to mine. But at the time, in that ticking house, with girls giggling and rain rilling down the windows, Julian's argument made perfect sense.

"Point," I answered.

He showed me a bathroom so I could change.

In total, I spent maybe ten minutes in that house. Even so, I should have clearer memories. I know there was a strip of tan or gray floor-covering that ran the length of the hall. It crackled when I walked on it and felt stringy on my bare feet, like beach matting. Something about the expanse of wall suggested generations of family pictures that should have blanketed it. But I saw only a few photographs, mostly of two tow-headed girls at various ages, shot from behind or far away, splashing in water, tumbling down dunes, bundled in scarves and stacked on top of each other on a toboggan as they sailed down a slope as white as these walls must once have been. The photographs weren't in rows and had been hung crookedly in cheap frames that glinted in the low light like half-buried shells.

I lingered a few moments in that ticking hall, stealing glances—that's what it felt like—up the stairs into the house's hidden upstairs heart. I imagined skylights, beds with white duvets tucked into eaves. The carpeting on the stairs was the same dull blue as the entryway walls. Julian had returned to the front door or never left it. In that light, he looked blue, too.

The girls were already outside, trundling towels and flippers and sand tools down the drive in a wagon. I don't know why I expected them to be younger, frail and bedraggled Julian-kids. These were gawky, long-legged tweens, trotting out of their yard toward their ocean, giggling and shoving, bending abruptly to birds or animals in the bushes, thwacking each other with towels. White-yellow hair bounced on their bare backs, which were New England-pale despite the time they clearly spent in the sun.

Or rain.

"Sorry," Julian said. "Can only keep 'em penned so long."

"No reason to pen them for me. They don't know me." And won't, I thought. That was true, but why think it?

"I'm so glad you're here," Julian murmured, pulling the screen shut behind us without locking it.

"You don't have to be that glad. I just came to make fun of you. Mr. Escape- Artist Flamenco Man, holed up from the world in the land of Living Tuna."

"There's still world out there?" He said it lightly. The inflection I hear now is one I put there.

The walk proved short, maybe a quarter mile back down that frontage road, past those shady houses turned toward each other. The rain didn't so much tap the trees and tarmac as breathe over it. I got wet without feeling it, or without feeling different than when I was dry. Branches and bushes twitched all around. I'd probably glimpsed or sensed more living things on this walk, I remember thinking, than I did on my average workday sprint down crowded sidewalk to catch the 2 or 3. The houses, though, stayed motionless and silent, but not in any sort of peopleless way. They just seemed nestled in place, rooted as tree-trunks.

"Big dunes," I said, my gaze having slipped toward the water I couldn't yet see. The sand flowed so easily, almost liquidly out of the grass and neighborhood that I hadn't processed its height. These dunes were taller than me, high enough to obscure everything beyond them.

For some reason, Julian laughed. Ahead, the girls abandoned their wagon at the foot of a dune and vanished. I glanced at their dad, my old friend I hadn't seen in fifteen years, the man who'd brought flamenco to NW Noplace, disappeared, come back, disappeared, come back. Boom. He was still in the same shorts he'd had on when I drove up, same shapeless shirt. Rain slicked his skin without beading or running anywhere on him. As though sinking into sand, I thought, and finally, after all these years, realized what Julian's skin-tone was: literally, sand. This sand. Dune-color. He's even dune-shaped, I decided, in that way of dunes not quite having shape. Not the same shape, anyway, from one instant to the next.

Only when we came abreast of the wagon did I see where the girls had gone. A sandy path cut between two dunes fully twice my height, demarcated by ramshackle, red wooden fencing on either side. The path led to beach, wide and not quite white and empty. Beyond that lay ocean, slapping in white-tipped crosscurrents against the shore.

"Should we bring the wagon?" I asked Julian's back as he moved purposefully, almost eagerly down the path.

He turned, raising an eyebrow again as though just remembering I was there. "What for?"

From way off to the right, farther than seemed safe or even possible, one of Julian's girls shrieked. I hurried forward, realizing even as I did that Julian hadn't reacted. I caught up, and we cleared the dunes just in time to see both girls maybe hurtling down the strand, arms outstretched and heads thrown back, sailing over the surface of the water like seabirds before plunging into it.

They'd dropped their towels in a heap near more red fencing that jutted a surprising way out onto the beach, almost to the water's edge. Beyond it, I was surprised to see a curve of green hillside ringing the edge of the bay—I decided it was a bay—wreathed in mist. It was hard to tell how far that hillside stretched. Far, though; another full-on peninsula, and in the mist, I saw houses, white and palatial, like docked ocean liners.

Not rooted, I thought, with no context or source for the thought. "Who lives there?" I heard myself ask.

Again, Julian's answer was to some other question. "They have their own beach."

"What beach is this?"

"Slough. What's left."

Unless he meant What's Left. It could have been the beach's nickname. Or full name. What's Left Beach. Unless it was a self-abnegating joke, or a comment on land erosion. Julian was proving as tough to pin down as he'd ever been, even in conversation. Asking him questions was like talking to rain.

I almost tripped over the old woman.

I hadn't seen her, or anyone. Suddenly my foot caught in sand or discarded sandal, and I almost toppled into the laps of a white-haired couple I swear must have crawled out of the earth like crabs. There'd been no one there, then there was, and they almost had me. Hands out, stumbling and apologizing and swearing, I staggered sideways and somehow kept my feet.

"Sorry," I breathed, got steady, glanced down. Instinctively, my hands flew to my chest where at least one of my cameras generally hung.

How the fuck did she get here, I thought, and only when Julian greeted her, said some name other than "Dr. Tilley" did I realize it wasn't her. This woman didn't even look like her once I got a clearer view: too rumpled, stick-thin. Same shock of hair, same startling sparkle in the eyes, I guess, but that was it. Just another old woman who'd sucked something juicy out of life and retained it, somehow. There was no other resemblance.

Her husband—brother, manservant, how do I know?—looked surprisingly burly, broad-shouldered, his pectorals heavy, only slightly saggy, like folded sails. But the sand had sunk a little more underneath him, or he'd settled more deeply into it. That, more than anything else, is what suggested the Tilleys to me: his strength, subservient to her regal, straight back. Sand dotted them all over, coating their legs and abdomens, as though they really had been buried in it. The thought should have been funny, and was, but only momentarily.

Not crabs clawing out of the beach at all.

Foxes by their burrow.

"Wet one today," Julian said, eyes on the bobbing blond heads of his girls in the water.

"Might go all week," the old man answered.

The woman sighed. I've never heard a more serene sigh. "Suits me," she said.

It wasn't her voice that jolted me. It sure as hell wasn't that sigh. It may have been the way she kept her hands buried to the wrists in What's Left Beach, never once glancing at the hillside houses or Julian or me. Or it may not have been anything to do with her. But what I heard in those two words was, Fuck you all.

"Friends of yours?" I muttered as we moved away.

"Known them my whole life," Julian said. Not quite answering. Again.

That's where I'd gotten Fuck you all, I realized. She'd known Julian his whole life, never once seen me. Hadn't asked. Wasn't interested.

Closer to the water, the clouds lowered still more over the bay like the lid of an aquarium. I wasn't actually considering swimming. I hadn't swum in years, probably since Daniel and I moved to New York. As a kid, during summers, I'd jumped off a low, disused railroad bridge with a few other girls into a way-too-shallow river. Our very own poor-kid, What's Left River. Swimming had never drawn me much.

But now I experienced an unexpected moment of dread. Mostly because it had been a seriously long time since I'd seen Julian's girls.

Grabbing at his hand, I raked the surface of the bay with my gaze. I saw nothing for what felt like a full minute, and that's counting from after I'd noticed.

"Julian, fuck, where…"

Girl One, the elder, popped up way out to sea, half-turned toward us, like a sleek blond whale breaching. She vanished again just as Girl Two surfaced much closer to shore, rose halfway into the air, and sank.

"Coming?" Julian said, kicking off his flip-flops and moving fast, seemingly keeping himself from running only by force of will.

"I think I'll just—"

"You're already wet. Keep me company." He grinned wide and guileless. "I never have company."

Dropping my towel, not quite shaking my dread or managing to stop my eyes from darting around for another reassuring glimpse of girl, I followed. Inanely, I remembered some lifeguard admonition from the one summer of sleepaway camp my parents had managed to afford: Never, ever swim alone. Of course, I wasn't alone. I wished for my phone so I could text Daniel anyway.

By the time my toes touched water, Julian was waist deep, sinking fast. Rain slid down him. Girl Two popped up startlingly close, splashed him, and kicked away and under. Glancing back, I saw dunes, the fenced stretch of all but empty beach, the old couple wavering in the drizzle. The second old couple—white-haired woman, this one in some kind of bonnet, guy in a panama hat with a cigar drooping so far out of his mouth it looked like an icicle—just spreading towels and joining them.

Without meaning to, I edged farther from shore. The bay climbed over my knees, splashed at my thighs. Except when looking straight down at my waist, I couldn't even tell where my submersion point was. Not only was everything wet, everything was the same clammy warm: air, bay, skin, rain, Lori's black bathing suit, which hung heavy and surprisingly hard like a turtle shell. Something closing over or growing out of me.

I didn't like it. I turned to wade out.

She hit me—Julian's daughter, one of them—just hard enough to knock me off balance. I swore as I fell, submerged momentarily, felt bottom and stood. I couldn't have been under for more than a second. Just long enough for sensations to slam me.

The sound: shells rolling, water slapping and popping, Girl Two's laughter, which I couldn't really have heard and did, streaming around her, filling the bay.

The scratching, as if Girl Two had raked me as she knocked me over. But there were no marks. What I'd felt was just her skin. Scaly sandpaper. Like a shark's.

The single glimpse: blond hair, long body wriggling effortlessly away. Vanishing. The way sharks do.

Scrabbling to get my feet under me, I stood, swayed there streaming in the rain. I couldn't see Julian or his children, just gray water and sky knitting together. A more perfect union scrolled nonsensically through my head. If I turned, I thought—I knew—the beach would be gone. The fence, the dunes, the old couple. Couples. I was Noplace, but for real, this time. I'd grown up somewhere that had never really been its own place, a half-suburb of a not-quite-urb. This had been somewhere, though. A region.

Colony.

Country.

It wasn't now. Was barely an appendage.

Julian popped up straight ahead, smiling wide. My feckless flamenco-friend, streaming. Melting. He beckoned. I didn't want to come, stepped forward anyway. I felt myself sinking. Mirroring him as he lowered toward the water. I went under when he did. That's how I finally saw them.

Or did I?

What did I see? How could I have?

They were fifteen feet away, maybe more, far enough that I shouldn't—couldn't—have seen anything.

And yet I was scrabbling, half-screaming as my feet flailed for sand to stand on. I vaulted up, gasping for breath as though I'd been held under, near-drowned. Turning, I kept jerking my head down, tensing to leap if one of those girls suddenly eeled around me, bumped me again. I was watching the water, not the beach, so I didn't see everyone else until I was already back on land.

I never stopped moving. I'm sure of that. Mostly, I'm sure of that because I'm still here. Still me. I don't know what that means. I never have. I just know it's true.

Questions bombarded me, poured down like rainwater.

Where had they all come from? When? How long had I been under?

They were in a sort of semi-circle, not really a formation. All on their beach towels, and not all of them old. Spread across the sand like an extended family to watch fireworks. One spindle-armed, pointy-shaped girl—not Cindy from the Land of Living Tuna, it didn't even look like Cindy, any more than any of these people looked like Dr. Tilley, except in the way they all did—even had a bag of marshmallows. Or something squishy. She kept sticking in her fist, squeezing, then lifting and licking the goo from between her fingers. Laughing.

The old couple I'd seen first still sat on their blankets. Instinctively, I lurched to the right to skirt them. Which meant having to dart between the towels of two other families. At the time, I was just praying, clenching my hands, silently begging them not to lunge for me, to let me go.

But in retrospect, I'd almost rather they had lunged. What they did instead was ignore me. As though I wasn't there. As though I never had been.

Nevertheless, I almost leapt as I crossed the barrier they hadn't exactly created, then fled between the dunes back to the road.

Running back to Julian's took too long. Impossibly long. Like the drive from Providence, and that whole, insane day. Houses seemingly lurched closer to the street, leaning over their own leaning fences. But no tenants stepped from doorways. Rain shadows moved in curtained windows, but no curtains stirred. Maybe everyone was on the beach, I thought. Still, I kept my eyes on those porches. It was better than blinking, which would have meant seeing the bay. Seeing beneath it.

I almost didn't go back into Julian's house. I'd already wrenched open the car door when I remembered my clothes and keys.

I didn't hesitate, just threw myself through the unlatched screen. Move, I was snarling in my head. But for one second, I stopped. I had no idea where to go. I whirled, half-expecting to find Julian and his girls floating in mid-air, snaking up the drive. But they weren't out there.

They're already in you, I thought, ripping abruptly at the leaden straps of Lori's bathing suit, which had gone on solidifying and gaining weight like lava hardening, land forming. It took agonizing seconds to shed it, and when I kicked into motion, I did so in intentionally jerky lunges and hops because I didn't want to fall into rhythm with the ticking. Those clocks. How many fucking clocks were there? I still only saw the one, but felt and heard the rest, on the other sides of walls in rooms I never went. Forming a fairy ring, like redwood trees make around the dead space where something mighty and towering and old had spawned them and died.

I was almost sobbing by the time I found my clothes neatly folded together, keys and phone on top. I considered just grabbing them and fleeing naked into the rain. But I got myself calm enough to dress. Staring the whole time out the open door.

At some point during that mad, hours-long drive back, I stopped to text Daniel. Two points, actually, or else I texted while driving. Daniel showed me when I got home. I have no memory of sending either.

The first reads, One if by land.

The second, For the land, and of it.

For it and of it.

Daniel still pulls up those texts sometimes, whenever he catches me feeling competent. He still wants me to explain.

Sometimes, I try. I tell him they're about the way Dr. Tilley made me feel. The thing I almost understood, for that one day, about the nature of her hate.

Sometimes I tell him they're about why Julian always went home.

Mostly, I say I don't know. That's closest to true. That whole day hangs in my mind like a memory from early childhood, something assembled out of a series of days over a period of years and embellished with elements that weren't there, bits of things I was told, other people's memories. It's not real, or it's not reachable.

Except for what I saw under water. That memory stays imprinted. That single moment when I opened my eyes to the bay and saw them, Julian and his girls, half-concealed half-disclosed, shining in the swirl and streaming gray light. Disintegrating like sand sculptures. Breaking up into the billion particles and old bits of dead things that made them up, the intrinsic impulses and old hatreds that would ground and sustain them for as long as they were them, then lay down with them in the gloom of their graves. I watched them wave in the deep like flags.

I will never know if it was one silver fish or a school that they had trapped between them. I will never know if they were playing or bare-hand fishing or hunting. Toying with prey like a pod of orcas as they swirled around, darted in, swirled back.

If they had hands, they were holding them. If they had eyes, they were watching what they'd trapped, not me. The only thing I'm certain they all still had—the only thing that had stayed on their faces—was mouths. Their desperate, hungry, wide-open mouths.

Julian and his girls, from What's Left Beach. From that land and of it, whether they wanted to be or not—whether we want them to be or not—forever drawn back to their beginnings. To their house full of clocks their slaves made them.

I will never even know if they were laughing or screaming.

DestinationLand

I mean, of course there were ghosts. The place may as well have been constructed to house them. All those hulking, hollowed-out things that had once traversed the country, packed with goods and people and breath and noise and smoke and movement. Silent, now, and stilled, rescued from scrapyards and brought here and posed in the brittle, baked grass at the shadowless end of Rogers Park like some sort of haphazard railroad Stonehenge. They lured bored grandkids or summer camp field-trippers who climbed all over them, yanked the levers that still moved and most of the ones that didn't, made screeching smokestack sounds, poked in the empty coal bins, leaned out the windows of the engineers' cabs to stare down tracks that were also only for show, led nowhere. Eventually—usually after only an hour or two, certainly by mid-day—the kids would get tired, sweaty, and they'd climb down and let their sweating, exhausted counselors or babysitters read the plaques alongside each engine or caboose, or make up stories if they had energy left to dream.

DestinationLand. Dumb name. If there are any places on this planet *less* about the destination and more about the journey, I'm betting they have clergy.

Also an insanely insensitive name, given Rogers Park's history and reputation. Very few of the interred Japanese who'd died at (or survived) the abandoned camp back in the hollow on the other side of the hills behind the

Round House, or the vanished migrant kids or kidnap and murder victims reputedly buried there, had wound up in this place by choice.

Mostly just dumb, though. At least, that's what I thought until the day the Wong kid came.

I'd been coming for weeks. Maybe more. I'd been laid off again, so I volunteered to drive my Aunt Frida to DestinationLand on Tuesday and Friday afternoons. I'd walk her to what she called the Round House, which was in reality the little gift shop shed fronting the working turntable she and her buddies— Coal-Black Neil, Flat-Cap Phil, and the Hobo, an actual billionaire—had constructed to shunt engines and cabooses into the work area for their monthly hosing down. Off the little group would toddle to tighten bolts or hammer heat-warped ties back into shape or slap a new coat of paint on the latest decommissioned or decrepit trolley or coal car donated by some municipality or failed freight line or museum. Meanwhile, I parked myself at the splintery picnic tables along the back fence that fronted the freeway to scroll through Want Ads and Craigslist on my phone, and occasionally wander over to watch my aunt and her Ancient Order of Railway Elves fix things. There wasn't any shade anywhere in that flat, dusty expanse, but at least I could *see* shade up under the walnut trees on the hillsides that separated DestinationLand from the rest of the park.

Hot, prickly days. The only wind came from trucks passing in the slow lane of the freeway, but the roar was constant; if you closed your eyes, you really could imagine you were in motion. I don't ever remember the park being crowded, and even though the visitors were mostly kids, they never made much noise, just climbed on the trains, went still for a while to stand on viewing platforms or stare from glassless windows, then rose up like grasshoppers and ticked over to the next car.

There were only ten, maybe twelve of those in total, in various stages of disrepair despite the Ancient Order's constant efforts. The two wooden passenger cars had been salvaged from a long defunct Pasadena-to-somewhere excursion line. Families could—and, amazingly, did—rent those out for birthday parties on weekends, even though they got so hot by midday that

I half-expected them to sprout smokestacks, sound whistles, and light out for one last zombie-train junket. Alongside those was a grim, gray-slatted freight car with deep dents all over its metal frame. According to its plaque, which no one read, its final cargo had been tenant farmers lured from South Carolina tobacco fields to work the steel mills the striking white laborers of Pittsburgh wouldn't. There'd been a battle, the text read. Massacre, I presume. The dents came from that, and the Ancient Order let them be.

My Aunt Frida's favorite was the Bird of Paradise, a mirror-ceilinged, art-deco dining coach, the only surviving remnant of a train that somehow plunged off a bridge over Sidewinder Gorge near Death Valley in 1937. The third worst railway disaster in California history. Forty-three dead. When rescue teams arrived at the scene, they found the rest of the cars and everyone in them obliterated on the rocks below, but the Bird of Paradise perched above, dangling its front wheels over the edge of the track. "Cocky, like," according to an observer in one newspaper report amid the collection encased in a glass case in the Round House. "Like she'd pushed the rest of them over."

As for the cabooses, the Ancient Order kept those sparkling clean, bright red and yellow, and kids poured into and over them all day long like bees on snapdragons. There was one double-welled grain car, the only thing in the whole park I never saw a single person climb or even pay attention to.

Finally, of course, there were the engines. The biggest towered just to the right of my picnic table at the back of the park, set apart from everything else, seemingly grazing there like a bull commanding a pasture. It didn't have any friendly Thomas the Tank Engine face painted on it. Its only color was black. But it *gleamed*. It had to have been twenty feet high at the tip of its stack, and whatever rust or decay had wormed through that thing, it hid it well. Its actual name, according to Frida, was a number. BX47 or something like that. She also called it Ceres, or possibly *a* Ceres. But everyone else at DestinationLand just called it the Lord of the Prairie.

The days settled into a pattern. Frida liked to arrive no later than 7:30— "to beat the heat", though to do that, we actually would have to had to get there by 3:00 a.m., or maybe February—and off she and the Elves went to hose and hammer. By 9:00, the first half-full buses of Scouts or YMCA campers appeared, and kids would line up at the entrance and then, released by their minders, erupt over the park like butterflies shaken free of a net. There'd be bursts of shouting, Spanglish, laughter, pushing and shoving, but soon the heat and the spell of the place got them, and they'd settle on or near their cabooses or engines of choice and stare blankly and pull things. Flit onward. Circle back.

Around 10:30, the freeway traffic sometimes thinned enough that you could hear canned calliope music from the carousel in the next field over, and whatever dew the grass had left in it burned away in a slow, streaming mist that pooled along tracks and crept under the wheels of the trains as though seeking somewhere to die. On the quietest days—meaning, the hottest— I could even hear the ponies trudging down their dirt track in the Pet-and-Ride paddock next to the carousel. I wandered over there once or twice, but the sight of those snuffling, fly-ridden creatures just made me sad. Reminded me of me, if I was feeling particularly pessimistic about my current state of affairs. Except at least they *had* jobs. Still, they made me think of ghosts in reverse, fairy-tale beings conjured off their gleaming merry-go-round poles and reanimated and forced to plod back and forth across the dirt and their own manure in the merciless sunlight. The only hope I could generate for them was that the children constantly being strapped onto or pulled off their backs were less annoying than the gnats and silvery crawling things infesting their manes, burrowing under their saddle straps to gnaw at their bellies.

Definitely better to be a train.

The first families—a few tourists, but mostly locals as far as I could tell, lots of retirees without the patience or heart or money for another sweaty slog through the zoo but needing *something* to do with the grandkids—appeared mid-morning, which was the busiest time. The popcorn cart near the Round House opened at 11, mixing a whole new oily odor into the wafts of exhaust fumes and banana-scented sunscreen. The carousel gave the whole scene a ghostly, far-away soundtrack. Finally, promptly at noon, the Little Prowler shrieked itself awake.

The Prowler was DestinationLand's one and only original, its lone train birthed in captivity. The Ancient Order had constructed it entirely from scrap metal and laid the tracks for it over a period of years. The goal was to give the place one actual ride, and also to raise money for the rest of the restoration work.

In reality, of course, it wasn't even a train. Not a real one. It did run on tracks, out of DestinationLand into the shadowy valley around back of the nearest hills, all the way to the sycamores under which lay the razed foundations of the Japanese internment camp, then along the zoo's perimeter fence and through a little stone tunnel before returning in a long, winding loop to Destination Station. It had an engine, a sort of desiccated-pony version of the Lord of the Prairie, and seven squat blue open passenger "cars" that looked like shopping cart baskets, each with facing benches to seat a family of four. But its fuel was diesel, not steam. It had a smokestack, but all that spewed from it was fumes that funneled back over the riders. Really, the Little Prowler was a tractor. You turned it on with a key.

I never once saw it completely full. But it ran all day, and fast enough to cut the heat or at least stir it. In motion, at least from my picnic table, it did generate a sort of magic. The Elves took hour-long shifts driving her, three twelve-minute excursions per hour. The designated driver would step up beside the engine, turn toward the sweating throng of maybe three families on Destination Station platform, collect tickets, then yell "ALLLLLLL ABOARD, next stop…"

Different outbound destination every time. Driver's discretion. Chicago. Mexico City. Madagascar. Sometimes the passengers got to pick. One time, I heard Frida yell, "ALLLLLL ABOARD, for Sea of Tranquility," and it gave me the shivers. I don't know why.

When the train came back, the engineer of the moment would climb out, call, "DESTINATION STATION, doors open on the left", and the dazed families would clamber off. I told Frida once that they should have tickets printed saying DESTINATION: DESTINATION. She didn't see why I thought that was funny. I didn't either after I said it.

I only rode the Little Prowler once. Until the last time, I mean. I liked it more than I thought I would. The motion—or maybe the stupor brought on by the diesel fumes—took me out of myself, away from money panic and general wasted-life malaise. Up front, I could see Frida's kinked, white hair spilling out of her engineer's cap like uncoiled industrial wire. She loved driving that train, in no smart part because she'd helped build it. I liked my Aunt Frida, always had. When we were kids, her backyard was an enchanted world full of tilting but sturdy homemade swing sets and jungle gyms with hidden crawl-tunnels and pirate ship enclosures. The Island of Lost Cousins, as my mom called it. Whatever else Frida's life had dealt her (and it dealt her plenty), she had made herself useful.

The train slipped into the shadowy valley, which wasn't really cooler but *looked* cooler, anyway. Up on the hill, walnut trees stood so still in the breezeless air that they might as well have been painted there. Part of the construction. Our motion was steady, the light soft. We curled past the sycamores, those sad slabs of cracked cement foundation in the grass, and around to the zoo fence. I was hoping to see elephants, buffalo, maybe the big cat enclosure. Instead, our view got blocked by the reptile house. Right as we hit the tunnel, I did hear gibbons, though. Or maybe birds. Jungle birds, from somewhere else.

The tunnel was tiny, and served mostly to smother our faces in fumes, as though we were being chloroformed. But then came a moment, right as we emerged. Abruptly, there was the sunlight again, and track cutting through the long, untended grass. I had just a few seconds of…I don't know. Not looking out a train window, but looking out the fogged-over memory of looking out a train window. If I even had any actual memories of doing that. Then we were back in DestinationLand.

Usually, by mid-afternoon, movement in the park had dwindled to occasional escorted trips from picnic table or caboose to the bathrooms or maybe the popcorn cart for cold water bottles. By 4:30, when the half-hour-to-closing whistle sounded, there was never more than a handful of visitors left. At 4:45, the Engineer appeared.

Every day, 4:45 on the dot. Shine or shine.

I never saw him arrive; he always seemed to be stepping from around back of the Lord of the Prairie. *Like a hobo*, I thought more than once, watching him make his slow, lurching way from the big engine toward the Round House. He couldn't have come from there, really, unless he got into Rogers Park by hopping the freeway wall every day. But that's almost always where I saw him. Blue pinstriped cap, pulled low. Spindly arms in a greasy, blue button-up shirt, untucked. Clean jeans spilling down to canvas Vans the color of the dirt in the park, worn without socks. Ankles the exact same color as the shoes and the dirt.

Same time, every time. At some point during my second or third Friday in the park, he glanced my way, and I winced. *For* him, not because of him. His sunburn looked positively baked into his face, fiery red and peppered with pustules, like a relief map of the park on fire.

Blue eyes. Smile that looked like it hurt as it slashed through all that redness.

From then on, he waved every time he saw me. His gait was steady and jerky at the same time. That is, jerky but in a steady manner. *Like a train's*, I remember thinking, watching him move through the families packing up, the kids climbing down from the Bird of Paradise or the cabooses. I never saw him speak to any of the Ancient Order, but they had to have watched for him, because every day, one of them would meet him at the Round House and escort or just walk with him to the Little Prowler. Then whichever Elf it was—usually Frida or Coal-Black Neil—would turn back toward the last stragglers in the park and give the call.

"Ladies and gentleman, we have reached our destination. All passengers please disembark at this time. Thank you for visiting, and if you're able, please do leave a donation in the box as you leave so that we can keep this magical place open and all these noble trains in the condition to which they are accustomed."

Meanwhile, the Engineer would climb into the cab of the Little Prowler, sound the whistle, and turn the key. Off the empty little train would go for its last ride of the evening.

Always empty. Park tradition.

I never asked how that tradition started. It didn't seem to matter, was simply how days ended in DestinationLand. Part of the routine and the quiet magic of the place, which I understood was at least as important for guys like the Engineer—and old people like my aunt and her friends—as it was for the kids or their minders. You know those old tabletop automated dioramas they had in arcades a long, long time ago? The really big ones? Put a nickel in the slot, watch all the weathervanes on the little farmhouses twitch, the barn doors snap open, little metal horses spilling out to slide down slots into the corral to bob their heads up and down in the felt grass? The whole thing built to scale, the fences painted so precisely that you could see flecks and flaky spots? Cotton ball clouds floating overhead, their shadows the exact right size, surfacing in the landscape at precisely the correct angle? The miniature sheep on the hillsides moving just enough to be moving, their wool shivering in no wind?

DestinationLand always reminded me of one of those. Made me feel like every one of us had our separate track, and the blazing desert sun was the nickel in the slot that set us into slow, circumscribed motion. Same motions every day, lasting exactly the same amount of time, slowing and finally stilling at the exact onset of evening.

Until the day the Wong girl bolted through the just-opened gates.

There's the first difference, right there. Not the bolting, lots of kids did that at the moment of arrival. The lull of the place, dictated by the heat and the aura of the trains themselves, took a while to get in them.

But the first arrivals were almost always campers, and came on buses. Boys and Girls Clubs, Scout troops. The Wong girl sprinted in alone, glancing over her shoulder just long enough to yell "*Come on!*" Her grandmother appeared a good minute later, leaning on her cane, already sweating. She stopped at the edge of the first tracks, visibly struggling for breath. The girl circled back and barreled into her, threw her thin arms around the grandmother's waist, and the grandmother laughed. Held onto the kid. The girl turned, dark braid banging against her back like the tongue of a just-rung bell, arms akimbo. The two of them surveyed DestinationLand together, taking in the Round House, the cabooses, the Bird of Paradise, the passenger cars and popcorn cart, the Lord of the Prairie. Slowly, after a surprisingly long time, the kid nodded.

"Now, *that's* a place," she said. Then she shot off again.

The grandmother took up station at the picnic table next to mine. That whole day, we watched together. The woman smiled the entire time. Couldn't seem to stop. I kept stealing glances, feeling oddly drawn to her. She had a wide gap in her top front teeth, like a tunnel, but if she'd ever been self-conscious about that, she wasn't now. I don't know why I kept looking at her. She often looked back, was generous with that smile. At some point, she introduced to herself as Mrs. Wong. The widow Wong. There was something *nourishing* in that face. Or nourished. A happy face, in spite of life. I remember thinking that I hadn't seen so many of those.

Frida's, most of the time. A couple counselors or parents I'd noted in this park this summer. Very few others.

The Wongs stayed all day. That was another difference. DestinationLand really did cast a spell, could mesmerize even the twitchiest kids for hours. But not indefinitely. The Wong girl didn't just climb the cars, either. She read the plaques. Came darting back to the picnic table to tell the tales or ask what tenant farmers and Pinkertons were. She disappeared into the cabooses, reappeared in the engine cabs. Pulled every lever, stared out every window. At least four times, she got her grandmother off the bench to ride the Little Prowler. Later, sometime after lunch, I spotted her by the fence surrounding the work yard, watching the Elves. Then she was talking to the Elves. Then my aunt had given her a hammer, and they were kneeling together at the splintered front grille of some decrepit red engine the park had recently acquired, touching and tapping at it together like blacksmiths shoeing a horse.

When the Engineer appeared, I was startled, thought he was way early, then realized it really was 4:45. That a whole day had gone by. That the widow Wong had fallen asleep at the table next to mine, her head curled down into her collar like a cat's. And that the girl herself had vanished.

That fact alone shouldn't have propelled me to my feet. What would even be strange about temporarily losing track of that kid?

But there really was something about her. The movements, the plaque reading and questions, the darting and climbing all around. As though a one-child Monarch swarm had swept down on DestinationLand. Colored it brighter.

Attracted attention.

That was what alarmed me, I think. The reputation— the *history*—of Rogers Park. And the gleam off that kid. My eyes flicked back and forth from the Lord of the Prairie to the cabooses to the Round House.

She's in the work yard, I told myself. *Frida has her.*

But Frida didn't. In fact, at that moment, Frida was arm in arm with the Engineer, moving at the old man's lumbering pace around the front rim of the giant turntable to the Little Prowler for his daily ride. I headed for the Elf Enclosure, peered through the chicken wire, saw Flat-Cap Phil and the Hobo packing up tools. The Hobo noticed me, lifted his Sprite can and shook it. Offering me one, I realized. His Rolex, diamond-studded, winked through its days-deep coating of dust.

Spinning back toward the park, I stared at each of the Little Prowler's cars as the last kids climbed from them. There were hardly any other children about. The buses had been gone for hours, as usual, to beat the worst of the traffic. I smelled popcorn, sunbaked metal, a hint of manure on the wisp of breeze from the pathetic ponies over by the carousel, diesel from the Prowler idling at its station.

"*Ladies and gentleman, we have reached our destination,*" I heard Frida call, in what I only then recognized as the old-woman version of a voice I'd loved all my life. The sound of summer. Of the Island of Lost Cousins.

Except that on Frida's island, the cousins always came back. As opposed to this park.

The harder my heart banged, the more ridiculous I felt. The Wong girl wasn't my kid. Was almost certainly fine. Was probably already shaking her grandmother awake, chattering them both toward an on-the-way-home waffle cone.

But she wasn't. The widow Wong was where I'd left her, had in fact sagged forward onto her folded elbows as though melting into the picnic table. My eyes flew around the park again: cabooses, Bird of Paradise, Lord of the Prairie. Behind me, the Prowler let loose its leaving-now shriek, and I whirled, and I saw her.

Saw her shoe, anyway. One red Ked, poking just a little out the open side of the back car of the train because of the way the girl was crouching there. I couldn't see her face, and yet I could already imagine her grin. I'd been seeing it that whole day, after all. Less mischievous than alert. Ready for adventure wherever she found it.

Like being the first-ever passenger on the Little Prowler's last ride of the day. Even as I thought that, I saw her dark braid appear over the rim of the car as she took her first peek, and the train sighed into motion

What I did next was instinctive. Stupid. Also not-a-kid clumsy. I could have shouted, flagged the train to a stop. At the very least, I could have alerted Frida, who was already disappearing back into the Elf Enclosure to pack away her tools. Instead, I took three racing steps and leapt into the car in front of the startled Wong girl, barking my shin hard against the frame of the train and then banging my elbow on the metal seat as I dropped to a crouch in front of her.

For a second, all I could think was how hard my shin hurt. My eyes filled with tears, and my vision with shooting meteors of pain-light. The kid had squeaked when I leapt on board, and also vanished back down under the rim of her car. The pain dulled a little. I started to sit up, and caught sight of the last of DestinationLand sliding past as the Prowler picked up speed. Shadows seemed to unclip themselves from the hillsides and drop off the walnut trees like sheets from a clothesline. Surprisingly cool air blew over and through me. Suddenly, I didn't want to sit up. Didn't want to be seen. Didn't want the Engineer to stop the train and put us off. Ever.

"Hey," I said into the metal divider between my car and the kid's. I said it louder, kind of yell-whispering, then realized that was ridiculous. There were five empty cars between us and the grunting, rumbling diesel engine. Probably, the Engineer had already seen us. But he couldn't possibly hear us. The third time I said "Hey," I did it in my normal voice, and the kid answered.

"I have a cellphone," she hissed. "I already texted my Gram where I am."

The only answer I could think to that was, "I have one, too."

New shadows rippled around the car, as though we were a wave passing through them. Sunset was hours away, but on this side of the hill, twilight had come, nestling in the trees and actual, green grass—weeds, ice-plant, whatever, it was alive and green—rolling right up to the edge of the tracks on both sides.

Eventually, through the dividing wall, the kid said, "What are you doing here?"

My answer came instantly, and with a smile. "Same as you." It was almost true, I realized. Sure, I'd wanted to make sure this kid was safe, got back to her Gram. But I'd also wanted a forbidden train ride. Ten or so glorious minutes in motion, with no one on Earth knowing where I was.

My knees had locked, which made it hard to straighten them. My shin had a big, bleeding scrape down the right side. Every time I inhaled, my nostrils filled with diesel fumes.

But the breeze we made poured through my hair and down my back, cooling my skin. My eyes, so used to combatting the ruthless sun, released their squint, and softer light filled them. Those next few seconds were the best of the summer. I opened my mouth to let loose a laugh, and noticed our speed decreasing. The air-brakes hissing as the train slowed. Slowed more.

"Shit," I stage-whispered, ducking my head beneath the rim of the car. "Stay still." Then, to my surprise, I laughed. The girl did, too. I told her to shush.

"You shush."

As if we were playing hide and seek. As if the only thing that would happen if we got caught is that we'd be it. *And get to drive the train*! I thought nonsensically, right as the Prowler rocked to a stop.

Had the Engineer seen us? I figured he must have, was about to make his lurching way back here. That thought wasn't nearly as fun as the ones leading up to it. I realized I was holding my breath. The fumes felt slick, liquid in my mouth, as though sucked from a siphon. Cicadas screeked all around. The sparrows and purple finches that had scored my last few months all sounded together now, dozens of them from up in the trees or off in the scrub and chapparal, as if marking the hour. Or raising the alarm.

"*Sssh*," the girl whispered again. Possibly to the birds.

The train rocked. Not hard.

Temblor? *The Engineer climbing down, holding on to the cars as he inched toward us*? But it hadn't felt quite like any of those things, and the rocking settled almost as soon as it started. When the whistle went off, the girl squeaked again. I think I did, too, and I definitely banged my knee against the front of my car as I jerked in place. The motor rumbled back to life. Another shriek of the whistle, and we were moving once more.

At the second stop—a little longer than the first, at the foot of a squat coast live oak whose roots spread wide, dug deep into the dusty ground like talons—the rocking felt harder. Lasted a little longer. Only after we were moving again did I register what that movement really reminded me of:

Not the Engineer clambering down. Other riders climbing *on*.

Straightening my aching knee, I glanced up and saw that the Wong girl had already snuck just enough of her face over the top of the metal divide so she could see the rest of the train. Her eyes widened, and her breath whistled as she gasped and ducked back out of sight.

"What?" I said.

Her shush this time was more violent, but I ignored it. "*What?*"

She didn't answer. Out the sides of the cars, dusk had deepened on the hillsides, surprisingly fast, as though a tunnel were coalescing around us out of empty air. The greenness on the ground surged like the surface of a sea woken by wind. Or stirred from below.

I couldn't help it. Twisting to face forward, I eased up on my haunches and lifted my head.

At first, I didn't...that is, I wasn't...Even now, I'm not sure what I actually saw. The train, obviously, hurtling ahead (except not actually hurtling, we couldn't have been going more than ten miles an hour, but it felt like hurtling, or maybe just *looked* like it). Up on the hills, the twilight glowed orange at the edges, as though the sunset had burnt it. The cars in front of us juddered, rocking as we moved.

I ducked back down hard, banging my cheek on the divider in front. Then I sat with my throbbing head in my hands, rocking to the rumble of the train, trying to make sense of any of it.

All those heads, tilting left and right above the seatbacks like tethered balloons. Barely above the seatbacks, though. Like children on school buses, bobbing around as everyone batted at each other. Shouted at each other. Fought. Sang.

Except I'd neither heard nor observed any of those things. Now that we were fully in motion again, I couldn't even hear cicadas or birds. Wind, either, because we weren't moving fast enough to make any.

Also, if there were really children on the train, how had I still been able to see the Engineer? Because I had indeed seen him. The back of his head, anyway. Along with the tops of every seatback and every car divider between us and him.

As though there was nothing else on the Little Prowler at all.

The third time we stopped, the engine shut down. Immediately, bird and bug noises flooded over us as though released from a dam, filling our cars, the train, the whole valley. Way up front, rocking started again. Metal groaned. Then more rocking, but closer.

As the cars filled. As children climbed on.

There aren't enough seats, I thought abruptly, wrenching around, staring out the side of my car.

Whatever I was expecting, I only saw hillside. No children. No empty air shaped like children.

The engine shuddered back to life, spitting diesel fumes into the evening. Right as we rumbled into motion again, I really did I think I heard something else for the first time, though from far away. It could have been school-bus laughter and singing. It could also have been the carousel from over the hill.

I didn't want to speak or move or make any sound of my own. But I also didn't want to be where we were the next time the Prowler stopped.

Not if someone else needed these seats.

"Hey," I said, as low as I thought I could and still be heard. When I got no answer, I closed my eyes and said it louder.

The girl's voice came back lower than mine, but loud and clear. "Mister..."

Too late. Already, we were slowing. Stopping. Stopped.

I didn't then, but now I know where we were. Way back in the valley by that grove of protected sycamores, near the foundations of the razed barracks from the Japanese internment camp.

We could have jumped off right at that moment. If the Wong girl had leapt, I certainly would have followed. I think if I'd gone, she'd have done the same. But I couldn't still couldn't make myself move. And whether the girl also couldn't or was waiting for me, she didn't, either.

Everything was quieter, there. Not silent, but these were different birds around us now, night creatures calling hellos to the dark. Even the cicadas seemed to have settled, relaxing into their small-hour pulse, steady as water over stone. *Screak-screak-screak-screak.*

I'd been holding tight to the top of the metal divider, breathing silent, waiting for more rocking. But when it came, it was different.

These were the sounds—this the motion—of riders getting *off*.

I wanted to look. So badly. A part of me even wanted to stand up, take the Wong girl's hand, step out, and introduce ourselves to whoever they were. Just so we could see what they were doing.

But in my brain, I kept seeing what I'd seen before, and also not seen: the backs of heads. The Engineer's head over but also through them.

That's why I didn't even straighten my legs again until we finally started moving. The Little Prowler accelerated— if that's the word—back to cruising speed and started its slow circle toward the zoo fence, the tunnel, Destination Station. When I did lift my eyes, the first thing I saw was the Wong girl, because of course she was already up. Already looking.

"Now, *that's* a place," I heard her say for the second time, even more fervently than she had this morning.

I turned.

There they were. Not so many of them, really. I can't give an exact number, can't even really estimate, because mostly I saw flickers. They emitted no light, but their shadows stirred the tree shadows, caught what ambient light there was. It was the rhythm of their motion, more than anything, that reminded me of fireflies in hedges. There might have been ten, total. There might have been dozens. It was impossible to tell. But almost all of them were small. Child-sized.

All those children.

What were they doing?

I still wonder, all the time. Were they setting out a picnic? Preparing for a round of ghost in the graveyard with the barrack foundations as base? Just gathering, as they maybe did and still do every single night at that hour, or whenever the Prowler crawls by to pick them up? All those kids for whom the world had no use—or, worse, the most monstrous and terrible use?

On nights the Prowler doesn't come, do they walk? Glide?

All I know for sure is the pulse and flicker of those shadows, which made me think of the pitiful ponies in their paddock, released from their yolks for the evening to graze together on whatever brittle shoots of night-grass they could find. Then I thought of carousel horses climbing down off their poles, communing on their platform under the stars with the music quiet, the sun gone, no one to see them. No one to ride them. Nothing to carry but the weight of the dark.

Ten seconds, tops, I knelt there staring. Probably less. For just those seconds, it seemed so peaceful. Right up until one of those shadows turned, and saw us.

That's still the only word that comes to mind: *saw*. It was looking, I felt it.

I couldn't actually see its eyes. If it had eyes.

But it saw.

Beneath our feet, the train shuddered, started to slow, right as the shadows—*all* of them, not as one, but together, like a pride of hunting lions—poured off those razed foundations, out of the shade of the sycamores into the grass.

Toward us. Fast.

Even in the instant, I wondered what they wanted. To avenge? Overrun? Subsume? *Play?*

Assuming, of course, that what I saw was anything like what I'd decided they were.

Whirling, I saw the tunnel. Two thoughts crashed together in my head: I didn't want to meet whatever this train picked up in there; and I didn't want the shadows to catch us. Especially not in the tunnel.

"Jump," I snarled, grabbing for the Wong girl's hand. But she was already in mid-air, out the zoo side of the train, stumbling as she landed and then scrabbling along the little berm that ran between the fence and the back side of the tunnel. That seemed completely the wrong direction to me, but I followed, almost smacked face-first into the chicken wire as I tripped, caught myself, then lunged off after the kid.

What made her jump out that *side? Was that what saved us?*

By the time I caught up, she was duckwalking along the berm, steadying herself with her hands against the curving stone of the tunnel. Already, the structure blocked our sight of the rest of the valley, and there wasn't any grass back there, just hard, crusted dirt—*was* that *what saved us?*—and so for a few seconds we just worked our way down the structure, across ground no actual person had likely trod in decades. I did notice the sudden absence of sound. No birds, no engine rumble, no far-off calliope or whisper of wind. As though we'd leapt into an airlock.

I could still smell diesel, though.

Right as we reached the far end of the tunnel—ahead of the Prowler, it hadn't emerged—I felt rumbling under my hands. I also felt it in the earth. The train restarting. The dirt bubbling underfoot. I didn't see or hear either of those things, they were just what the sensations suggested to me. I grabbed the girl, who squealed, quite probably because she was scared of *me*, and I thought again of those flitting shadows. All the kidnap victims and abandoned migrants and homeless and Japanese and battered wives and God knows who else who'd vanished here. Wound up here.

Maybe even the people who died on the trains the Elves had brought here?

Despite the girl's squirming, I held her tight until the Prowler passed. It couldn't really have been going fast. But I swear I felt its wind, and it seemed to erupt from the tunnel as though newly born—*re*born—and race away across the swirling, surging grass. All I saw of the Engineer was the blur of his too-red face, the wind pouring through the stringy gray hair under his hat but not lifting it. Not even stirring it. As though it wasn't even there.

The ripples in the grass had broken away from us to follow the train. *Maybe we lost them,* I almost said, but even I wasn't sure what I meant. I loosened my grip on the girl's arm, but also whispered, "Wait." She tensed like she was going to run but stayed put. I don't know what she saw, never asked. I was too busy counting to 100. As if we really were playing ghosts in the graveyard. Whatever game this was, though, I really, really didn't want to be 'it'.

Ninety-eight. Ninety-nine.

"Okay, straight down the tracks," I murmured.

We could have cut across the grass. But that seemed like a bad plan. The kid bolted right where I'd directed, toward the mouth of the valley and the freeway noise we could suddenly hear again, loud and clear. Toward DestinationLand.

It stunned me how little time it took to get back. We were running, the grass around us (or whatever was in it) eddying, doubling over itself, circling back, but by then we were at the edge of the fencing around the Elves' enclosure, and then we were in the park, on the platform, standing in the heat still pouring down out of that burnt orange sky. The Prowler had already settled into its spot at the far end of the station and shut down. As I watched, hands on my knees, breathing hard, my aunt appeared, offering an arm to help the Engineer—stumbling, locust-limbed old man—climb from his perch.

They moved off together, slow as those ponies in their paddock, across the dust, past the Round House and the popcorn cart toward the parking lot. The Wong girl, of course, never stopped running, and she threw herself into her the arms of her relieved Gram, who made cooing, clucking grandmother noises and engulfed her.

Only once, right at the park entrance, did the Engineer look back.

He had eyes. Of course he did. But he might as well not have.

Why did I think that? What did I even mean? I didn't know then, don't now. And anyway, it wasn't really his eyes, but his movements, jerky and repetitive as an animatronic Disney pirate's as he moved on his rounds—down his tracks—to his train. To pick up his passengers as they rose from the ground or floated out of the walnut trees. To take them on *their* rounds.

Because he was one of them. Performed the exact same movements, at the same pace, at the same time. Every single day.

Just like Flat-Cap Phil. Coal-Black Neil. The Hobo. The ponies in the paddock. My aunt.

Breath spasmed in my throat, burst out of me in a cough. I kept coughing, couldn't seem to get enough air as my thoughts went wild. *When, exactly, was the last time I'd seen Frida except on our way to or from this park? Just how many of the denizens of DestinationLand had reached their destination?*

Not the Wong girl, or her grandmother either. There they were hurrying from the park, the girl already pointing at something new, laughing again. The grandmother slower, but not lurching, her gaze riveted to that girl, as far from blank as any human gaze ever gets.

Which just left me. Standing there thinking back on my summer, which had lasted how long, now? All those hours on my bench by the freeway near the Lord of the Prairie. Scrolling the Want Ads but never finding anything. Watching the ponies in the paddock, the Elves in their enclosure, the Prowler on its rounds. Smelling the popcorn and diesel in the air.

Every Tuesday. Every Friday.

And the other days? Where, exactly, did I go, then?

A Paradise to Live In or See

B y 7:00 a.m., the trailer was an oven, and Jodi had thrown on cut-offs and her **Motherhood is Always Having to Say You're Sorry** t-shirt and stumbled outside. The shirt, still damp from the sink-wash she'd given it the night before, cleaved to her skin and sealed in the heat. She honestly couldn't tell anymore when she was sweating or just wet.

For a few seconds, she stood in the gravel with her glass of too-warm sun tea, listening to crows fighting in the lot's lone cypress and watching the dirt driveway bake. Eventually, she tried again to adjust the SunBrella she'd bought, "New in Pak!", for fifty cents at the Goodwill going-out-of-business sale up on Foothill the month before. As usual, it wouldn't open all the way, and also tilted too far to the right or left on its plastic base instead of staying centered. If she kept repositioning it, and no wind kicked up, and she crouched in just the right spot, she sometimes could earn shade in five-minute intervals. Later this morning, she suspected she'd be doing exactly that. Her latest version of her favorite pastime: surviving it.

For now, though, she set down her glass, tied back the ball of dried kelp she called her hair, and did a three-minute, barefoot tree pose right there in the dust, next to the barrel cactus, so that if she so much as wobbled, she'd pay for it. Beneath her, earth seemed to crack, disintegrate into specks spilling over and through each other. *Like larvae*, she thought, didn't wobble, held her pose. At three minutes, she shifted legs. Only when she'd finished did she let herself turn, for the first time that day, to the gate behind her trailer.

"Good morning, Joy," she said to the barbed wire atop it. Beyond the cyclone fence, the long dirt "lane"—the Bastard actually called it a lane—furrowed past the single scorched palm, through dead mesquite, and around the collapsing hovel the Bastard referred to as his mansion to the back field. There, amid the spiny vine and hip-high black mustard weed that sloped down to the concrete barrier that bordered the 210 Freeway, sat two roofless sheds, the shot-out school bus where the Bastard let his current harem stay, and the rusting silver Airstream where Jodi's daughter lived with Stump. Her newest, stupidest man.

Jodi knew all this because the Bastard had let her in to see it exactly once. Let her stay just long enough to brand it into her memory. Then, in a moment of inspiration, he'd locked her out again—"just until Joy instructs me otherwise. She's my tenant, after all"—but told Jodi she could park in the driveway as long as she liked.

"Bastard," Joy had snapped as he clicked shut the padlock.

"That's my name, babe. Don't wear it out." He'd shot her that fucking gap-toothed, jack-o'-lantern grin. He was missing even more teeth than Jodi remembered, and his gums had gone a sickly, mushy orange that seemed to be seeping into his cheeks and chin. Full-blown pumpkin. Rotting one.

To her own amazement, Jodi had realized she didn't hate him. You couldn't hate him. He didn't hate her. If anyone had asked, he'd probably have said he was glad she'd gotten her shit together. Gotten out.

Only now, of course, she was back. For a second, in that moment, it felt like she'd had something more to say to him. Or, even stranger, that they had something to say to each other. But the moment passed. He'd sighed, rubbed a hand across his beard like a rake through ashes and left a streak. Off he'd moved toward his hovel. The filth in the air that swarmed this whole area—this entire, unincorporated nowhere between old meth-alley Tujunga and the asphalt manufacturing plants and empty used car lots of northern Pacoima—seemed to hover around him, move with him like

Pigpen's cloud of dirt in *Peanuts* cartoons. As if the horror that was himself was a halo.

If a breeze ever actually came, she'd thought, he'd just flake away. But none did.

"Thanks," she'd called, on impulse. Then wanted to vomit at herself. He hadn't even turned around, just disappeared into that horrible house.

Months ago, now.

Finished with her stretches, Jodi considered just driving away, as she did every morning. She could leave a note with an email address pinned to the gate. Or not. She'd tried so hard, done what she could—which, admittedly, amounted pretty much to parking out here— and kept doing it.

But what had that made up for or healed or solved? Nothing.

Across the street, the Mexican girls appeared on the stoop of their shack, their backpacks absurd on their shoulders, bulgy and blocky, like saddlebags on ponies. One of them called something over her shoulder that sounded like "puta" but might have been "pooch," or "Oops." Then, together, they started their usual slow walk down the block to their school. Possibly, the Bastard owned their shack, too. Also maybe their mom.

"Hola," Jodi called.

The older girl, maybe nine, glanced up. Sometimes she did that. Occasionally, she said hello back. Today, she flipped Jodi the bird. Birds. Both fingers.

Jodi laughed.

She would never leave this spot. Not until Joy did. Whenever that happened, wherever Joy went next, Jodi would follow. She'd park her camper as close to wherever her daughter landed as property boundaries allowed. Personally deliver take out. Keep fresh-brewed sun tea and two glasses waiting at all times. Run over Stump with the camper the second Joy finally came to her senses and asked.

Maybe before then.

Around back of the Bastard's hovel, down the hill, truck brakes screeched on the freeway, triggering more brake screeches, a whole chorus. Like giant atomic mutant crickets greeting the dawn. No crash of crumpling metal today, though. Yet. No screaming. No sirens.

But in the hedges that lined the driveway and ran all the way back into the Bastard's field, the dead shrubs surged. Crackled. Most likely that was the raccoons that sometimes clambered over Jodi's camper roof at night. Probably, sooner or later, they'd find their way in. Help themselves to her Cheerios.

Or maybe there was a fire?

A mom can dream, Jodi thought. Certainly, the filth in the air had gotten into the shrubs, too, hovering in the gray, ashy branches like smoke and making them look like they were simultaneously disintegrating and taking shape. In the process of being sketched, but also erased.

Automatically, her fingers found the roach in the pocket of her cutoffs. Barely enough left to fit in her fingers. But here it was at her lips and lit, the actions so conditioned and efficient that she couldn't remember doing them, any more than she could drawing breath. Which she was doing now, along with the acrid smoke from the stub, which did nothing to mask the stench of this place. Mesquite and exhaust fumes. Creosote and coyote shit and ozone and new skunk spray. All of it singed, perpetually on the edge of burning, or already burning just out of sight like those underground coal fires that never go out. Or one of the wildfires erupting almost every day now, up and down the state, just over the next ridge or a thousand miles away.

She sucked in a last hit, and only then remembered where she'd gotten the joint in the first place. From fucking Stump, who'd tossed it over the barbed wire to her. *As a peace offering? A taunt? A test initiated by Joy? Was she supposed to resist?*

And let the Bastard's undeniably first-class shit go to waste?

Sometimes, with her eyes closed and the smoke in her, the freeway really did sound like ocean.

"Good morning, M.O.M.," Joy said, right behind her, so close that for a second Jodi thought her daughter had come out from behind the fence, was going to allow a hug. She whirled, eyes flying open and arms rising.

But her daughter was where she always was, on the rare occasions she let Jodi see her. In the Bastard's yard. The heavy curls she'd inherited from Jodi still glowed vibrant and red as they spilled down her shoulders, but her face looked ashen. The eyes hard as coals.

M.O.M. Mom of Mediocrity. Joy's name for Jodi for as long as Jodi could remember. Once, in the middle of a particularly awful screaming fight right before Joy left for good, Jodi had pointed out that "Mom of Mediocrity" actually implied that *Joy* was the mediocre one. And Joy had responded by doing the most damaging, hurtful thing possible: stood there, teared up, and nodded.

I've failed. Again, Jodi thought now. Wordlessly, she handed the joint through the fence to her daughter, who took it. Wordlessly. Sucked the very last smoke from it, staring past Jodi at the street or maybe the horizon.

Actually, Jodi realized—the realization as startling as it was comforting—Joy looked kind of good. Almost. Steady on her bare feet in her smock-dress, and clear-eyed. Familiar with the morning. The weight of another day she could face on her shoulders.

Even as Jodi thought that, though, her daughter shuddered, and her eyes flicked toward the Bastard's house. The shudder, of course, could have been shakes. Withdrawal. From whatever. Voluntary or otherwise.

"He even in there?" Jodi asked. Careful, casual, like they did this every day. Neighbors in their yards. Mother and daughter. "Haven't seen him in a while."

The last of the shudder made Joy's shrug look spastic. "Me either. He brought me scrambled eggs last week."

Nothing surprising about that. His usual method of baiting and hooking. And keeping. "Big of him."

"Hash, too."

"Obviously."

Joy scowled, tried flicking the sucked-out roach away, but it shattered to dust in her fingers instead. "Corned beef hash. He made it himself."

"Really?"

"Said if I gave any to Stump, he'd shoot Stump's legs out."

That *was* surprising. "Good on the Bastard."

"He *hates* Stump."

"Really good on the Bastard," Jodi murmured, but regretted it instantly. She waited for Joy to tell her to fuck off and stalk away. Plus, now that she considered it, maybe none of this was so good on the Bastard after all. It had always been part of his thing: dangling his keeplings over the lip of the escape he always claimed to want for them.

At least Joy hadn't flipped her off yet. Might even have nodded? *Had that been a nod? Was this the morning? If I just up and asked, right now? Said, 'Come on, love of my life, least mediocre thing I've ever done. Let's just go...'*

It was too soon, and Jodi knew it. This detente too new and fragile. But here was her voice asking anyway. "Joy, please listen, *please* don't fight me, what if we just—"

"You know the back of his house doesn't even have walls anymore?" She wasn't cutting Jodi off. She hadn't even been paying attention.

By the time Jodi realized what her daughter was talking about, Joy had gone on.

"Since the last fire. Instead of rebuilding, he just cleared the rubble away. Sort of, mostly he just pushed it down the hill into that fucking pool. So now, it's like one of those cabañas or whatever in the Bahamas. Those ocean houses on stilts? Except without stilts, obviously. And instead of ocean, it overlooks..."

Possibly, Joy's latest shudder started well before her voice trailed away. Was still the last of the shakes from before. But when it passed, she sagged momentarily into the fence, which creaked beneath her weight, conformed to her shape like some fucked-up, meth-country hammock.

"What?" Jodi finally asked, as softly as she knew how.

"Just...don't let him invite you swimming."

"Want to come over for breakfast?" It was hopeless, Jodi knew. She kept on anyway. "Poach you eggs? I have strawberries." Which was true. Every Thursday and Sunday, Jodi walked two miles each way past the asphalt plants, through the vacant lots to the Farmer's Market to get whatever they had, but strawberries especially. Joy's favorite. At least, they had been back when Jodi was sure she knew such things. On impulse, through clenched teeth, she added, "You can bring Stump." And then, because she couldn't help it, "Assuming you can wake him."

"Fuck off, M.O.M.," murmured Joy, without heat but also without affection. Hoisting herself off the fence, she turned away, gaze shifting toward the hedges that bordered the Bastard's lane. The Easternmost edge of her current world.

"I'm sorry. Joy, wait. Please."

"Relax. I'm just going to get a wrap."

A wrap? Because she was cold! As always.

Which meant she was coming??

Squaring her shoulders as though prepping a Warrior pose, forcing herself to breathe, Jodi somehow kept her voice level. "Okay. Great! I'll just go start…"

In the corner of her eye, she saw the parked cop car at the bottom of the driveway—realized it had been there, *here*, all morning-- a split second before the gunfire erupted.

So much gunfire, a burst thunderhead that kept bursting. Automatically, Jodi threw herself at the fence, flung up her arms to climb toward her daughter and immediately impaled one palm on a twist of barb. Someone—*her, definitely her*—was already screaming. Shouting "*JOY!*" over and over, barely audible even to herself over the barrage. Somehow, she'd got off the ground, and now she was dangling from the spikes in her palm while balancing on the balls of her feet, which she'd jammed into two small diamonds of chicken wire.

"*DOWN,*" screamed a new voice behind her, funneled and metallic. Voice-through-bullhorn. "*Get the fuck down! Oh, SHIT!*"

Instead, still screaming, Jodi yanked herself upward. Joy wasn't even there, anymore, and she wasn't crawling along the lane or sheltering in the hedge or sprinting for the Bastard's house.

At least she wasn't face-down dead in the dirt. Yet.

Of course not. She'd run for her goddamn Stump. Must have. Straight into the maelstrom.

"*Campbell, what the FUCK?*" shouted the cop voice from the driveway. "*Lady, Ms. Nole, get down now!*"

With a howl, Jodi heaved herself up more, felt spikes drive straight through the webbing at the base of her thumb. Instinctively, she ripped her hand outward. Blood boiled from the hole—*wound* was way too small a word, implied an opening that would one day close—and her palm flew to her lips, her mouth closing over the rip. Her own blood filled her mouth. Ahead, down the lane, the whole hedge rattled as though it had rats pouring through it. Which it quite possibly did. The shooting stopped. Whether that was good or bad, Jodi had no idea. The tears pouring down her cheeks felt even hotter than the blood on her tongue and teeth.

If they fucking killed my girl…

"Ms. Nole," pleaded the voice behind her, no longer through bullhorn. A young voice. Familiar.

Without dropping from the fence, Jodi swung her head around. Blood spilled from her lips, which made her feel like a wild thing caught feasting. Probably, that was exactly what she looked like.

"Please," said the officer. From the hedge, Jodi realized, that's why she couldn't see him. Officer Ortega, or something like that. He'd been out to see her a few times during her months-long camp—siege—on the Bastard's driveway, mostly to ask about Stump. The last two times, he'd brought her iced coffee and stayed a while, just talking.

Now he was hiding in the hedge. Scared to fucking death.

"If you kill my daughter, I'll kill all of you," she hissed.

The officer not only heard, he flinched hard enough to rattle the branches. "*CAMPBELL!*" he shouted abruptly.

Partner, Jodi figured. Whatever their plan had been, they'd royally fucked it. And now the one in the hedge was pleading with her some more.

"We just want him, Ms. Nole. Please come down. We just want to talk to him."

"You can have him."

"Not her. This has nothing to do with your daughter. Quick and easy…" His words trailed away. An echo from his morning briefing, where some cop genius had hatched this plan. If there'd even been a plan.

She could barely make out the officer's face. Brown, with that silly, stubbly mustache she'd started teasing him about the first time she met him. Younger than Joy, she realized. And yet already into his life. An actual sort of life, guns and all. How did so many people manage to wind up with one of those?

Ahead of her, the lane past the Bastard's house stayed empty, with just a haze floating over it. Gunsmoke, windblown dust, particulates from the freeway or the smog. All of it gray, flaking constantly into its component bits without ever disintegrating.

"Quick and easy," she hissed.

Beneath her, miraculously, the fence sagged forward like the hand of some giant, sky-borne god and lowered her toward the ground.

"Ms. Nole," called Officer Whatever, through the bullhorn again. The hedge along the lane crackled as something big blundered through it, fell against the fence.

"Oh my God," said the officer. "Oh, oh, *fuck!*"

Wounded palm jammed back between her lips, Jodi eased a leg over the tipping row of barbed spikes and tumbled onto the Bastard's land. The land gave beneath her as she fell, soft as one of those high jump landing cushions, except it wasn't cushiony. More boggy. Gross. She could feel—almost *see*—the dirt humping around her, scuttling over and down her. Scrabbling to her feet, she brushed hard at her t-shirt and shorts, smearing blood everywhere before dropping into a crouch and hurrying down the path.

To her left, the Bastard's house loomed, tilting and rotten, like a shipwreck that had snagged here decades ago. Most of the window openings still had glass in them, but the glass looked caked over, not just opaque but *crawling*. What would one even do with the days in a house like that? How would you…cook an egg? Sit at a tilting table and eat?

You should know, Jodi thought to herself. Snarled at herself. She'd haunted those sorts of places for years, after all. The entire decade of her twenties.

But she didn't know. Not really. If she ever had, she'd forgotten. Everything but sensations. Smells. The feel of floorboards like those under your feet, forever falling away.

"Joy!" she called, then ducked instinctively beside the scorched, dead palm. As if that skeletal thing could protect her from guns or the Bastard or Stump or any of it. She glanced up into the tree's crown, the blackened clusters of dead nuts dangling up there like wasp's nests. More likely, this tree would try to kill her, too.

The only movement from the Bastard's house seemed to be on the surface of those windows, and the wood of the walls. Haze slid down the sloping gray roof, overflowing the gutters, which were no doubt full of God even knew what. As she stared, a rat—maybe a squirrel, but probably not—poked a filthy face out of the nearest one, screeched, and darted away.

The Bastard wasn't in there. Couldn't be. Surely, if he were, he'd be raining automatic weapon-fire on anything that moved.

But if he was in there, and Joy was with him, she was probably safer than she'd be out here. The Bastard would keep her down and out of harm's way. From police bullets, at least.

Speaking of which…

Where were they?

The whole place—not just the Bastard's house but the path, the hedge, the driveway where Officer Whoever was hiding—had gone bizarrely quiet. In Jodi's experience, once the shooting started, it didn't end until it was over.

Also, she suddenly wasn't sure how much shooting there had *been*. In the moment, in her terror, it had seemed like bazooka barrage and lasted forever.

It had been loud, all right. But over really fast.

Nightmares erupted through her brain. One nightmare, really: Joy bleeding out, sprawled on the floor of Stump's Airstream.

Biting back a cry, she straightened, sucked again at her wound, and scuttled down the path. The Bastard's house seemed to lean after her on its molting foundations, less an immediate threat than an eternal one. Bored, decrepit lion in its long, gray grass, tracking her passing. For later. If it had the energy.

There were more trees back here, cypresses and scrawny oaks lining and leaning over the path, shivering in no wind, in blasts of truck exhaust from the freeway over the barrier at the back of the property. Their needles and leaves looked much more gray than green, their barks thin and pallid as old skin. And also *moving.* Not so much hollowed out by beetles as made of them. Crawling with them. Jodi kept catching herself holding her breath, waiting for the next bullhorn bellow to *get down.* Or the Bastard looming up in her path, flashing his pumpkin grin as he gathered her in. Or the bullets in her back that would finally put an end to all of it, for her. Leave her forever a few years, a hundred yards, and the right gesture short of home. Which was a place she'd never actually experienced, certainly never managed to create for her daughter.

Died trying. Best epitaph she could hope for.

Whipping her wounded hand to her face, she bit into the rip, screamed at the pain and the blood bursting on her lips. *Fuck you,* she thought, at herself. The world, too, but mostly herself.

Too soon, the cypresses fell away from the path, and she found herself in open field. *Field* in this case more category than actual description. Before her stretched a long swath of thigh-high, baked grass the color of cigar ash, flat at first and then sloping down toward the gray, cement wall that bordered the highway, which bellowed just out of sight, and sounded nothing like the ocean at all. More a volcano in its last heaving throes before eruption. Or the gates of hell.

Jodi never stopped moving. If anything, she moved faster. On her left, the marooned school bus coalesced out of the haze. It looked almost as gray as the grass, wheelless, tilting back towards the Bastard's house like a moon. The Bastard had set up similar living spaces in his Vegas compound back in Jodi's day, though he'd kept them in better condition. Repurposed U-Haul trailers, a discarded shipping container, a doorless panel van. In his pimping pomp, he'd even circled several of them around one of those hose-filled, four-foot-deep plastic wading pools, then had a suburbia-style pile of fake rocks placed at the front of the circle with a wooden sign he'd had made atop it: WHOREMEADOW ESTATES. He'd thought that was hilarious.

Jesus Christ, *she'd* thought it was hilarious. Partly—mostly—because she'd never quite descended to living there.

No. She'd been a house whore.

Another shudder, an involuntary glance back toward the Bastard's house. This time, despite her panic, the sight stopped her.

It really was *wide open*. Gaping. Not just windowless or doorless but wall-less on this side. The whole rear of the house had molted into the grass in a gray, wet-looking heap. The rooms inside still looked like rooms. In one, upstairs, Jodi noted a bed, made, with a table lamp. In the kitchen was a round kitchen table with a candlestick in the middle of it. Fat stick-candle still in it, but not lit.

Not abandoned, then. Which was worse, somehow. Made the house even worse.

"*Joy?*" she shouted. She didn't get an echo in response. Field grass crept over the open rim, invading more than sprouting. Shadows swirled on the stairs, curling toward the ceiling like blown smoke rings.

Or maybe down from *the ceiling? Or rising from the floorboards? Sliding off the walls?*

Movement to her left caught Jodi by surprise, and she ducked into a crouch as she swung toward the bus. She was expecting cops, Stump, gun muzzles. Instead, she saw a face at one of the windows. Pale, its milkweed-thin hair the color of the bus, the grass, the dead palm. Or maybe that was just the grime on the windows. Only the girl's eyes flashed actual color, a startling blue. Because they were peering over the top of the window, Jodi realized.

It was like looking in a mirror, and back thirty years.

"Oh, honey," Jodi heard herself call, straightening again. She was talking to this young woman, but also to her daughter. Maybe even to herself, now or then. As if any of them would listen. "Stay down."

Then, in her older, M.O.M. voice, "You fucking moron. Get out of here. Never come back."

In the next moment, she'd forgotten the girl completely. The bus, too, and the Bastard's house. Finally, she'd spotted the Airstream.

It sat maybe thirty yards away, down a steeper slope that than she'd expected, between two creosote bushes that couldn't have been tall enough to provide any shade but were certainly dense enough to house kangaroo rats. Or rattlesnakes.

Fucking idiot, she hissed inside herself as she started down the incline. She could still have been referring to her daughter, or herself, but she wasn't. *Fucking Stump.* She made herself go slow, though caution hardly seemed to matter at this point. Sandy earth slid under her feet, as though the whole surface of the planet was coming loose. A stink bug reared up in her path, and before she could alter course, she'd stepped on it. It popped like a grape, and Jodi caught a faint whiff of its insides. Defense mechanism. Old bologna left in the sun. Fat lot of good that had done it.

"Sorry," she murmured, got a clearer look at the Airstream, and stopped.

She'd expected bullet dents everywhere, and shot out windows. Quite possibly her daughter dying in the dust with her man cackling over her, or propping up Joy's body and using it for cover.

Instead, she saw an Airstream. Rusty, sure, but shinier than anything else on this lot. Still a little closer to silver than gray. Its lone door open, but no lights inside. The windows lowered but only one with its glass shattered, which could have happened anytime, not necessarily this morning. Might as well have come with the vehicle, it looked so natural.

But not the blood splattered all over the aluminum.

So much blood. Still wet, even in this ruthless sun. Sliding down both sides of the doorframe, streaked with something silvery and gelatinous, like an oil slick.

Stifling a sob, Jodi dropped low again into the brittle grass, but she never stopped moving. Scuttled closer. She knew she needed to keep her eyes on the glassless window, the open door. But her attention kept flicking to the blood. The way it slid and shone. The shine mostly from the gelatin atop it, swirling through it.

Brain? A gag rose in her throat, more panic than disgust. *But brain would be chunkier. Right? So.*

Eye? Exploded eye?

Even as she leapt, hands outstretched to grab the doorframe and propel herself inside, Jodi found herself marveling, just for a moment, at herself. Or really, just noticing. No matter what she was hurtling toward, now, she moved forward. Mom of Mediocrity, always and forever. But also Mom of Momentum, now.

She had her hands in the goo—which she'd expected to be warm, but turned out to be hot, boiling into the metal frame of the Airstream—and her face thrusting into the dark when something big blundered against her knees, knocking her sideways. Her face smacked into creosote bush, which raked her cheeks and jabbed down her shirt, but she ripped free instantly, got her feet under her and whirled with her pathetic fists already up, not to block, to fucking *punish*.

Then she stood, and she stared.

Then she laughed. Hardest, bitterest sound she'd ever had in her mouth. It tasted fantastic.

"Where's Joy?" she snarled.

At first, Jodi didn't think he'd heard. Maybe he couldn't, anymore. The movement Stump was making down there in the dust probably qualified as crawling. Certainly, he was on all fours in his shiny checkered boxers and RIDE THIS t-shirt, jerk-sliding forward with his head down, neck extended a little too far from his ridiculous, gym-humped shoulders. A toddler's crawl. Not even, actually; the movements were too oblivious, instinctive, pre-programmed. More desert tortoise. The big purple hole in his left arm puckered every time he put his hand down, squirting more blood into the crook of his elbow. The right arm wasn't bleeding, as far as Jodi could see, but it bent at a weird angle. Extra angle.

"Stump," Jodi snapped, stepping after him. She stood over him as he lurched, slid. Crawled. "Where's my fucking daughter?"

Stump didn't answer, but the field did. Seemed to. The grass stalks rattled, flaking wherever they touched each other. The freeway roar intensified like a wave rolling in. A prickle chased up Jodi's neck, and she spun, arms flying up again, but saw nothing. The harem bus, with no face at the window now. The dead palm tree. The Bastard's fucking house, which seemed to have sunk lower since she'd been by it, folding even deeper into itself. As though it were being swallowed by the ground. Or *was* ground. Forest rat nest.

Around it all hung that haze. Smoke from a fire she couldn't see. Or the particulates the sun set glowing every night at dusk, visible even in shade, now.

"Right in the fucking face!" Stump crowed abruptly. He'd gotten a good two feet in front of her while she'd had her head turned. "Ah, God. Right in the face."

With a single step, Jodi caught up, loomed over him. The temptation to slam her foot down, squash him stink bug-style, almost overwhelmed her. She wondered what kind of smell he'd emit. Up close, his skin looked cracked, sun-withered, like a lizard's. She was surprised there was any blood left in it.

"Where's Joy?" she asked again, raising her foot. If the fucker didn't answer...or maybe the second he did...

"In the face! *'Mr. Santorini, we have q warrant for your'*...BLAM!"

Lurch. Crawl.

"Stump. I'm not fucking kidding. Where's—"

"Right. In. The. Face."

Sirens strafed the air, seemingly bursting to life all at once. From beyond the Bastard's house, out on the driveway by her trailer, Jodi heard tires screeching, dozens of feet thudding into earth. She needed to move, she realized. Get out of the line of fire. Get Joy out.

Assuming Joy was still here somewhere. And alive.

This time, when she glanced back down, she was startled by how far Stump had gotten. His knees had given way, though; all he could do now was army-crawl on his elbows. The blood on his wounded arm looked thick as a coat of paint. And yet he kept crawling. He'd reached the steeper slope at the back of the lot, and his speed increased slightly as he inched downhill.

For one second—half a breath—Jodi experienced a moment of...not admiration, exactly. But kinship, of a truly terrible sort. Then she squashed that, hard and fast. Ignored the stink it emitted. In five fast steps, she'd drawn alongside Stump again.

"You heard the sirens, right? Asshole? You know that's for you."

"Help me," he said. Dragged forward. One elbow. The other. Paraplegic grasshopper with dust for veins.

"Ha. Fucker. I knew you were hearing me."

"Help me."

"Where's Joy?"

"Help."

In the hedges, and also back by the palm tree, everything rattled. The SWAT team, presumably, pouring over the fence, streaming through the brush, taking up stations instead of just swarming down here because they still believed there might be a threat.

Which there might be, she realized. Over her shoulder, the Bastard's house wobbled in its haze shroud, seemingly collapsing in slow motion, like a reversed film of itself being built. But no Bastard peered out its windows, and no automatic rifle array swiveled toward the police intruders. The walls—the *air*—was the only thing moving in there. And all it did was flake.

"Help," Stump chanted at her. Like the fucking Fly. "Help, help, help."

"Help you fucking *what*?" Jodi snapped, stepped toward him again, and finally saw the pool.

Actually, she smelt it first. All at once, in a sudden, sickening blast, as though a sewage drain had sprung not just a leak but a geyser. And erupted up through a paper mill, built over an abattoir.

Just...don't let him invite you swimming...

To fight down her nausea, Jodi glanced back the way they'd come. Stump's blood slicked the dirt like a fat, red arrow pointing right to him. It should have been funny.

That pool should have been funny. But it wasn't. Immediately wasn't.

Mouth pursed, hands swiping up and down her arms to shed perspiration or at least keep it from solidifying, Jodi stared. Tears, of all things, filmed her eyes. A gasp popped from between her lips, and the reek filled her lungs when she inhaled.

Was that *where Joy was hiding*?

Mostly, the pool was a trash heap. A cracked, concrete hole in the ground, surprisingly long, filled with black dirt instead of water, but also debris, as though from a flood. Tin cans. Fence wire. The two-legged, broken-off end of what might have been a dining room table. A lawn mower tilted on its side, half-sunken. Cigarette butts. Tent poles. Syringes. The top of a flamingo-colored surfboard sticking straight up out of the crud like a pink tombstone. A catcher's mitt. Slivered glass shards everywhere. Some forks sprinkled around like perverse, pronged wishing-well coins. Jodi found herself scanning for doll's heads, maybe a dog carcass.

Because they'd be reassuring, she realized. Signs of a sort of life-ruin she understood. Recognized as a life, ruined. Most familiar thing on Earth.

Then the whole thing heaved. Rippled as a wave shuddered through it, and all that shit in there shifted, sank lower, lost a little more shape. *Like mulch*, Jodi thought, didn't like that thought, staggered back a step with her arms up, definitely in protection mode this time. *From what, though*? Dropping to her haunches, hands in the dirt to hold onto the earth, she watched the ripples. The surge and slap.

Was there water *in there? Sewage runoff? Quicksand*?

Between her fingers, the ground felt crumbly, breaking apart at the slightest pressure into even smaller granules. The freeway roar, which had never quietened, surged again as some sort of truck convoy passed, the volume loud enough to *hurt* down here. But Jodi didn't lift her hands to her ears. She needed those to anchor herself. Keep between herself and that pool. Toward which Stump kept crawling.

Black film floated in globs across the surface, ringing and absorbing everything else. Tires, Jodi realized. Eventually. All of them seemingly melting on the bottom, losing shape, forming a slightly harder sheen atop the whole mess, like the skin of a pudding.

Even that rippled, though. Kept coming apart, reshaping. The particulates in the air, the drought-strangled, fire-ravaged grass, corpses of insects and animals, deck furniture and sand pails and beer cans, all churning around in that hole in the ground like bits of blasted boats in a harbor. In fucking Pompeii.

Or the La Brea Tar Pits. Where the bones and detritus of the *last* doomed age had bubbled back to the surface.

Before she'd considered it, without even thinking, Jodi was up, scuttling forward. Her eyes never for one second left the surface of the pool. "Stump!" she called, her voice barely audible even to herself over the freeway roar. "Get away from there."

He didn't look back or slow. If anything, he accelerated, or maybe just gave in to gravity. He had his arms pinned to his ribs, now, his bony ass swishing snakelike back and forth to propel him.

Behind her, Jodi heard bullhorn. Not the words being shouted, just the announcement shriek. Abruptly, she was upright, lunging downslope. Bullhorn voices rattled around her like warning shots.

"Stupid fucker!" she was shouting, at least as much at herself as Stump. How bad an M.O.M. must she have been to have her daughter's life wind up here? "Fucking *stop*!"

When she looked back, she saw cops pouring past the harem bus and across the lot. A big, black swarm of them, but still moving slow. Locust cloud of cops. She could make out words in the bullhorn roar, now. "*Hands.*" And "*Up.*" The stench—multiple stenches, battlefield smells, killing field smells—engulfed her, filling her mouth and lungs, so that every breath shoved them down deeper, spread them forever inside her.

"*Where's my daughter?*" Jodi shrieked. Almost, twice, she lost her footing, had to scrabble to keep from sprawling straight down into the morass, where this asshole actually apparently believed he could hide.

Right as she reached him, a yard at most from the lip of the pool, her foot rising to smash down on Stump's back and pin him in place, Jodi heard him laughing.

Laughing. A stupid twelve year-old's cackle. The sound of a shit kid throwing a bag of urine out a car window at some random passerby.

She could have stopped him. *Saved* him. For the cops to kill, or at least manhandle. But instead of driving her heel into his spine, she scrambled to a stop. Let him go.

He'd reached the rim. The curved metal rods propped there, which, insanely, really were the grips of a pool ladder, slimed with scum. This whole place a nightmare parody of backyard swimming. The end of swimming.

One last snake-butt wriggle, and Stump's forearm hit liquid. Jodi expected screaming. Melting.

What she actually saw—and felt—was worse.

It started in the ground. Beneath her feet, tiny pebbles and flakes of loose earth suddenly slid toward the pool. Because of the undertow. In the goddamn ground. The tug starting in the balls of her feet, then flashing up into her ankles, her shins, fierce enough that she fell back on her elbows, crab-walked upslope. She wanted to flip over, claw all the way back to the flat stretch of lot, and run. Right through the cop cloud and whatever hellstorm they were about to unleash.

But she couldn't take her eyes off the pool. The liquid in there sloshing crazily, slapping into itself all over the place like a riptide. And then, suddenly, snapping taut.

Gathering itself.

Stink jabbed between Jodi's clenched teeth, literally pried her open. She wasn't making any sound, was trying so hard not to breathe. But she couldn't seem to keep from watching.

The wave wasn't huge. Was just a wave, black and solid, rearing up mid-pool where no wave should have been, made—like all waves, she thought, the understanding making everything even worse, almost *natural*—of not one thing but millions, billions, the molecules that constituted silt or Earth crust or air or skin, bonding yet again. Taking new shape. Syringes and forks and glass glinted within it like broken seashells. And right in the curve—spread too wide, overrunning its outlines but still unmistakable—the Bastard's face. His molting, grinning, pumpkin face. For one second, Jodi even thought she saw arms, flung out in front of him like a bodysurfer's.

Black foam formed as the wave of slurry curled toward Stump. Who was still cackling, unless that was screaming. Ducking his head. Sliding into the muck even as it closed over him, the sludge slamming into the side of the pool and spattering greasy debris up the hillside, which immediately started sucking away again beneath her. Pulling back to gather anew, and the earth Jodi was clutching came loose in her hands, spilled down as she scrambled harder, and then she heard the shriek.

"*MOM!*"

That was all the ass kick she needed. Had ever needed. If she didn't get herself up, Joy was going to come down here. Flipping over on her hands and knees, Jodi jammed herself into the ground and yanked upward.

Moments later, she was in her daughter's arms on the lip of the slope, the two of them still and solid as stones as police poured around them and down toward the pool.

They stayed like that a long time. Holding each other. Not once did Jodi straighten, or look down. Joy wasn't looking either. Was too busy holding her mother, crying into her hair.

Maybe that kept Joy from hearing.

But Jodi heard. That *slurp,* overwhelming freeway roar, the helicopters overhead, the shouting policemen, as a little more of the golden west slid into the mire from which it sprang, along with the dire wolves that roamed it.

PART THREE

...from...

Tell Me When I Disappear

"All right, tents zipped, lights *out*!" Kerber shouts, and just like that, they're gone. All of them. Not the kids, obviously, the kids are still staggering out of the chemical toilets and making exaggerated vomiting sounds, spitting toothpaste any old where as they stroll through camp pitching sand or whipping frisbees at each other. But the rest of the adults--our colleagues—vanish in the dark like desert foxes, hole up in their own tents, wake their phones if they still have charge and can get signal, or just burrow into their sleeping bags on their air mattresses.

Leave us to it. Me and CFK. Which is only fair. We chose this duty.

I pop a watermelon mint in my mouth, watch the lights in the faculty tents bloom like night flowers. They won't stay on long. It's exhausting, chaperoning teens on anxiety-therapy trips to the desert. We're teachers, not naturalists. Didn't sign up for this, we like to complain. But of course we did. It's right there in the contract. Once a year. Every damn fall. I've never been sure these weeks do much for the children. But their parents sure love it.

Beneath my feet, the Earth rumbles. The flash comes a split second later, out of order, from the base of the mountains way off across the sandy emptiness—the Nothing With Teeth, as Steph used to call this whole place, or maybe the whole Mojave. The Marines at Twentynine Palms have been especially restive this week, dropping practice bombs pretty much every night, sometimes all night. Hardly surprising, I guess. So many possible wars to look forward to, now.

"Hey, Amelia," CFK stage-whispers. "Want to Blair Witch 'em?" He's standing astride the campground's two stone picnic tables, one foot on each, hands extended over the circular grill/firepit as if there's a fire there. Some years we do have fires there, every night, no matter who's on get-them-to-sleep duty, and all the adults stay out and huddle together and stargaze and talk. Share gum, shiver, complain, gossip. Remind one another to turn off Roaming so our phone charges last longer. Get the baseball score from Amy or CFK, because we're usually out here World Series week. It's not fun, exactly. But there's fun in it. A teaching life novelty, being at work but with adults and not at some mandatory meeting about dress code standards or lunch supervision guidelines or roleplaying SAFE (our district's latest behavior management acronym, for Steps to Avoid Flashpoint Episodes).

But the nights have been freezing this week, and the rangers don't want us or anyone lighting fires, anyway—too dry, too dangerous—and most of us are tired of talking. To anyone. Sick of each other, and the monster in the White House, and the murders of Black men climbing our feeds, and the constant smoke from the fires burning yet again upstate or out by the coast. Sun broiling all day, every day. This year, instead of just complaining nonstop about the chemical toilets at this campsite, the kids have been sneaking across the road and shitting in the cacti. Not even cleaning it up, then lying about it to our faces.

Not typical. Not in my experience. Not to *my* face. They know I like them too much.

I think I still do. But there's no doubt, something has shifted in me, too. In the country, and the Earth. Some nights, I swear I can smell it. Something even worse coming. Already loose in the air.

"Want a mint?" I say.

CFK jumps down and pads around the fire circle. I offer him my tin, and he scrabbles around in it with filthy fingers. His gym-rat shoulders ripple under the short-sleeved polo he insists on sporting no matter how cold it gets, even though I can see goosebumps atop goosebumps all over his skin. He's got his black wool beanie in his hands, and so I get a good look at just how bad his latest buzzcut is. As though the clippers kept slipping, skimming over patches. Possibly, he did it himself. Or else he ordered precisely this look at the super high-end male beauty salon I am confident he frequents. Both equally possible. Not even mutually exclusive, in his case.

C.F.K. I used to know what the C and F actually—no, *originally*—stood for. Saw it on some official looking reprimand notice from the district he left on the Faculty Center desk we share. But these days, to everyone who knows him (and to himself, I'm pretty sure), he's Crazy Fucking Kerber. As I watch, he bounces up and down beside me, either because he's cold or he's really itching to go terrify kids for fun.

His? Theirs?

He flexes his arms at nothing and no one. Certainly not at me. Sometimes, I still think he's a big, bouncy Labrador. Lots of bark, no bite. Sometimes, I think I know better. His Dartmouth PhD dissertation is on proto pan-sexualism in Edna St. Vincent Millay. I've read it.

"Now do you want to Blair Witch 'em?" he says.

Laughing, I lean back and catch some starlight in the burls of my fleece sweater-jacket. I imagine it pooling in the crags and ridges of my cheeks. Backs of my hands. My old lady hands. Not too many more of these trips for me. Gently—the way it mostly comes on me now, almost kindly, like a cat—the longing for Joe stirs. I wish he were the one here beside me, maybe even holding my old-lady hands. Or that he would be home when I got there. Or anywhere in this world.

On the other side of the little stand of mesquite bushes where the baby rattler was when we arrived this morning, as far back into this bowl of rock and away from chaperones as they can get, the kids are still circulating among their tents. They're flirting in their fluffy hats and pjs, or bent over cellphones, or clustering for safety with their friends, toothbrushes dangling from their lips like Joules. The ones actually sneaking vapes are back farther still, probably up *on* the rocks where they're not supposed to go, around behind boulders, feet brushing the mouths of snake burrows they'll hopefully never realize were there.

I sigh. "If we scare them, we're just going to rile them up."

"So?"

I shrug. "Okay with me. I've got nowhere to be."

As usual—though not always—he's all bark. He nods. "Should we put 'em down, then?"

The choice of words is artful. Intentional. Probably. He's doing it partly for my amusement. Definitely for his own. But that doesn't quite mean he doesn't mean it. Unless it does. CFK.

"If we try to get them settled now, you know we're just going to have to do it again in ten minutes."

"Half the fun."

"Let's give them their unaccosted minutes. These kids don't get many."

He takes another mint I didn't offer. Then he leaps back to the tabletop. *"IN YOUR FUCKING TENTS!"* he roars, and glances back my way, practically wagging his tail.

I don't reprimand. Don't say anything. My best and hardest-learned teacher trick. Human trick, really. I just lean into the starlight. He hops down again. For a lot more than ten minutes, we stand silent together and watch the night come out. The deer mice and kangaroo rats are already stealing into the mess area, hunting scraps. Dessert, actually. They've no doubt had their primary meals during the day, in the tents, rooting out the snacks the students are forbidden to have from unzipped backpacks and duffels while we were out scrambling or climbing. At our feet, the sand stirs, and two stink bugs and a scorpion surface like impossible alien submarines and lurch off about their moonlit business. Up on the nearest rocks, eyes glint here and there. Ground squirrels, probably. Ringtails. Even a desert fox or bobcat, maybe. Every now and then, in luckier years, we see one of those.

The Nothing with Eyes and Claws. Nothing with Spines. Nothing Camouflaged as Nothing. All ways Steph referred to the Mojave during the one week I knew her. I've never forgotten.

"Shit," says CFK, stepping forward, raising his right sneaker.

"Leave it be," I say, because I know him. Know this about him, anyway.

He lets it be, and I see it. Fat black tarantula bobbing along, almost floating over the sand like a jellyfish. This really has been the strangest year. Strangest trip.

The hiss jerks me ramrod straight. CFK hears it, too, whirls to stare with me into the mesquite stand.

"Didn't they catch it?" I say. Careful and calm, though I'll admit I don't love rattlesnakes. "I thought they caught it."

"They said they caught it." He sounds remarkably like a regular person for a second. Someone with healthy fears and appropriate responses to stimuli.

"The mom, too. Right?"

We'd had to call the rangers five minutes after our arrival this morning. Keep the kids on the sweltering bus, with the pissed-off driver glowering at them and growling at us that his vehicle was not a mobile home, he had places to be, and at the very least we better fucking silence our students. I got some of them playing heads-up for a while. That didn't calm the bus driver much, and in fairness it didn't lower the volume any, but at least it provided a distraction.

The rangers took over an hour to roust the snake. Not kill it, though I didn't see what they did with it. Move it, supposedly. Then its mom showed up. That was another, scarier hour.

Maybe that's why I keep thinking of Steph right now. She was the junior ranger enlisted to guide our hikes and boulder scrambles on my very first trip here. Maybe five years older than the students. She wore a floppy green sunhat and smiled all the time. The two key components of her disguise. I saw that right away. She saw that I saw. "Always remember," she'd told me at the end of our first campfire, after a good night, when all the other adults had turned in. "Everything here is trying to kill you."

She haunts me, sometimes. Steph. For years afterward, I'd asked other rangers who joined us if they'd heard from her. Knew where she was now, or what she was doing. Whether she'd made it, though I never quite asked that.

Most of them had no idea who she was. One guy shrugged and said, "Oh, yeah, her. She just vanished."

Another hiss, now. Except…not exactly a hiss. Maybe. It also seems farther away, the sound echoing from somewhere over by the rocks. CFK just stands next to me with his hands on his hips like he thinks he's Gary Cooper, mid-showdown. A split second from drawing. From this angle, I can still see the shadow of the black eye he came to campus with a month or so ago. He stomped past the open door of my room, already ten minutes late for his sunrise class, tie twisted sideways like a noose he'd slackened but not ripped free of, silk shirt buttoned wrong.

I didn't ask. Teacher trick.

As he went by, he scowled at me. But all he said was, "Amelia." And then, "Barfight."

Possible? Yes. But also possibly imagined. Or invented. That's *his* trick, of course. I've taught in the room adjacent to that man for fifteen years. I teach AP Psychology. I still have no idea. Whatever his mystique is, he's committed to it.

Gary Cooper or no, he's not moving to check around in the rocks. I move to stand shoulder to shoulder with him. Maybe one of us is reassuring the other. Wind kicks up, rips straight through my jacket and alpaca hat. My thin skin. Thinning hair. I mostly haven't minded getting old. Arthritis, stiffening of the spine, whitening hair, faces dragging along in my memory like cans on a newlywed's car—*Just Lived!*—mostly that has all seemed appropriate to me. In rhythm, part of the harmony.

But I'm definitely colder, now.

CFK digs an elbow into my ribs. "Okay, Mealie. Blair Witch time."

"Sure you don't want to roleplay some SAFE?"

"That's not even funny. Why would you even say that?"

"Because you called me 'Mealie'."

"You don't like it?"

"No."

"How's this for SAFE?"

Then he's off, clapping and shouting, pouring through the kids like a fox in a chicken yard. He barges right into a barrel cactus, roars louder, never even slows down. Shrieking, laughing—some of them are laughing—the kids dive for their tents. Hands in my pockets, I make my way carefully around the mesquite stand where the snakes were, across the sand toward the flags we've put up to divide the girls' and boys' sleeping zones.

At the flag line, I gently funnel the stream of girls tentward. Most of the ones still out don't even want to leave their tents during the day for fear of sand-scuffing their shoes. These girls are all pretty sure CFK's crazy is a threat for the boys, but flirting for them. If we were talking about any other teacher but him, I'd worry they were right.

Other years—every other year—even these girls tend to gather around me by this point in the evening. Ask me to tell them one of my stories, or do my night magic, or just sit and look at the stars with them. I'm the island they wash up on. A lot of them love it. I still love that they do.

But like I said: strange year. Most of these kids just stream past. One or two say "Good night, Ms. Joseph."

"Sleep well," I say back.

It's possible I hear the next thing wrong. I'm almost sure it comes from the group of three in the tent pitched nearest the flag line, all in matching pink pussycat hats, none of them in my classes. It's whispered, but not quietly.

"Cool your catheter, Granny."

I keep my hands in my pockets, my shoulders un-shrugged. Watch another twenty or so girls I'll never really know, or only know briefly on their way to becoming women I'll never meet, as they disappear into tents, switch on camping lanterns or ridiculously bright mag-lights that are going to lure any beetle or stinging thing in the vicinity. Another ten minutes, and I'll make the lights-out rounds.

"Ooh!" says another girl, just to my left. Jayna, from my class. "*Shit!*"

I whip around, scanning for snakes. But she's just standing with one foot in her tent, one out. I move toward her, but not as quickly as I should. *If she's got a rattler in her sleeping bag...*

"Did you see it, Ms. J?"

She has her arm up, finger jabbed at the horizon, and I abruptly realize I might have. A streak of light, way off in the far corner of my eye.

"Perseids," I say.

"Those come in summer."

Good kid, Jayna. On the spectrum somewhere. Nervous all the time, chattery but distant from her peers. Interested in things. "The rangers say you can still see them out here some autumns, on clear nights."

Nothing with Lights. Did Steph coin that one?

"I wish the sky were like this in L.A."

"Me, too, Kiddo."

We scan the heavens together. Automatic, after a shooting star. One of those experiences that instantly triggers longing for more. Like lots of experiences, I have learned. But with shooting stars, that longing is the very core of the thing. Almost the whole thing.

"I wish my sister were here," Jayna murmurs after a while, in a tone that suggests her sister isn't home, either. Is elsewhere.

I wish Joseph were here, I don't answer back. *And* my *sister. And my mom and dad.* I wish any of them were anywhere.

"Thanks, Ms. J," says Jayna, and I blink.

"For the shooting star?"

She laughs. Not even dutifully. "'Night." She ducks into her tent, and abruptly, I have to clamp my mouth shut and my elbows to my sides. To keep from shouting, *Snakes! Wait!*

At my feet, the sand stirs, slides over my shoes. Not like snakes. But like my feet aren't even there. Which is and always has been the way of the desert and everything in it. Another memory surfaces, from a long time ago. Fifteen years, at least. Possibly twenty. Somewhat younger me—on the outside, anyway, inside I feel the same, or think I do—with that year's Jayna, a whole trail group full of Jaynas, crouching around me in the dusk, all of us holding each other still as we watched a desert tortoise amble slowly, slowly past. One leg at a time rising as if cranked on some rusted winch under that beaten, sand-colored shell. One by one, in no order I remember making, we all crept forward for a closer look, loomed directly over the tortoise. Which took no notice.

The only desert tortoise I've seen in all these trips here.

"Oh my God," one of the pussycat girls says, laughing nasty. When I look that way, she's pointing *at me*, and oh, it's still so powerful, that tone and that gesture; it works on everything *not* a tortoise. I find myself wanting to check my sweatpants on my hips, straighten my glasses or what's left of my hair (as if that would do any good).

Except she's not actually pointing at but past me. With her fingerless glove. Pink pussycat paw.

"CFK!" she shouts.

Then all the girls are shrieking and giggling. Leaving me a tortoise once more, ambling quietly out of their lives. Out of life.

I turn and look.

He's by the trouble tent. Of course he is. Those boys have pitched their camp way closer to the rocks than they've been told they can go. The scatter of dirty socks and journals they will never write in and headlamps they refuse to wear and high-end thermoses their parents bought them encircles their area like a moat.

Not deep or wide enough, boys, I think, watching as CFK advances. Herds them before him. He's got his back to me, but I can hear him from here. The whole camp can. Trick of the rocks. Also of his. He's not even yelling.

"Want to stay up late? Is that what you're saying? Want to stay up late with me? I've got some fun we can have. Want to meet at the toilets? With your toothbrushes?"

"*CFK!!!*" calls another pussycat, but too loud, I know it even before CFK spins around.

He is good. He's easily 50 yards away. But the girl doesn't just go quiet; she ducks. He glances once around the whole camp, a prison searchlight on legs. "Anyone else want to meet me at the toilets?"

It's the contempt, I realize, that's so devastating. It might or might not be real. But it's all-encompassing, aimed at this whole experience and every kid here and every adult, too. Including me, probably. Himself, definitely.

Two minutes later, the boys are in their tents.

That next stretch of time can be magical, most trips. Almost as electrifying as slipping out of my own tent to brave the bathroom at 2:30 in the morning, the whole camp asleep, the moon gone and the stars everywhere, lining the sky in whirls and furrows. Seeded light.

Ironic, really. Those moments when I most doubt the importance we place on being "alive"—meaning, witnessing the universe at the expense of feeling part of it—are the ones I've been surest I was living.

Certainly since Joe died. Almost a decade ago, now.

Tonight, though, I can't get that pussycat girl's sneer out of my ears. I'm also finding CFK's act predictable. A tired show in its ten thousandth performance, there to be captured on cellphones and memed. How much did I ever really like it, anyway?

Also...

Everything here is trying to kill you.

All around me, I'm sensing if not quite seeing tiny faces peeking out of burrows. Overhead, just occasionally, I can hear the hunters that prey on them skimming by. The cacti scattered everywhere seem to twitch in the barely-there breeze as though signaling each other. From the base of the one nearest me, another scorpion scuttles out. I've gone whole years without seeing one, but this trip, they're everywhere. My least favorite desert animal, the creature I've been most sure would hurt me sooner or later. "Always check your sleeping bags," Steph warned our whole group, with that same smiling not-smile. As if checking sleeping bags is a thing you can do well by flashlight in the dark in a too-small tent. "Also your shoes when you put 'em back on. Scorpions like it warm."

CFK is sauntering my way, snarling warnings as he goes. Stomping out chatter, crawling things, whatever else he thinks needs stomping. Up on the rocks, the night shadows are creeping down. They always do, and I always wonder what, exactly, is up there to cast them. But tonight...I don't know.

They look wrong. Meaning, I think, that they look more like shadows of actual things. Long and spiny, causing little waterfalls of pebbles as they slide down. As if the sky has sprouted fingers. Gone hunting in the crags.

"Mealie!" CFK calls when he's close. Practically skipping. Labrador-CFK. He comes right up beside me. "Do the thing."

As though I'm a character in his show, I find myself starting to ask what he means. Pretending I don't know. Saying my line. Instead, I make myself smile.

"Hold still," I say.

He really does have wild eyes, dark yellow by starlight, like a bear's.

"Look at me." I don't really need to tell him that. Just part of the script. "Keep looking."

The key, Steph taught me, *is the wait. You have to wait. Let all the pathetic, insufficient tools we have for adjusting to the dark do what they can.*

"Okay," I say. When it's time. "Tell me when I disappear."

Very, very slowly, I slide right.

If I really thought back, I could probably remember her exact explanation. Rods, cones. The way our eyes sense movement or change as opposed to actual light in darkness. Or the other way around? But as with stars, tortoises, the miracle of sparked kids' interest, the discovery of stillness inside myself as my husband withered, I am more about the thing than the explanation of the thing. Though in the moment, I can love the explanation, too.

"*Rad*!" CFK whispers suddenly. "You're…" He starts to reach out, but stops. I am less than two feet from him, maybe fifteen degrees to his left. And, if we both hold still, completely invisible to him.

The scream ricochets around the campground like gunfire, sets off an avalanche of tent zippers coming down, heads popping out like tumbling boulders as I startle and CFK glares everywhere, hands flying up into guard position, as though whatever's happening, he's going to box it. At first, I don't know where to look. But then I spot the streak of pink, the glary pussycat girl stumbling back across the flag line with both hands at the tie of her purple sweatpants. Her cheeks glisten with tears. Or maybe sweat.

"He fucking grabbed me."

"Never even left my tent!" calls one of the asshole boys. Fletcher. The worst of them. He's all the way out, standing barefoot in the sand with his flashlight on himself. Bare gym-pumped chest, bare legs. Black boxers.

"You appear to have left it now," I say. Not yelling. I move toward the girl, leaving Fletcher to CFK.

He's already on his way. But not before yelling to the pussycat. "Course, if you'd stayed where you belonged…"

I flash a glare. Make sure he sees. I almost say it, because I'm really not sure he gets it, and I want the kids clear on what has happened. Even in the midst of the era we're in, CFK apparently still needs this explained to him.

But if he does, it's too late for him. And he's not my primary concern.

I reach the pussycat tent at the same time as the girl, put my hand out to touch her shoulder. "Come here, Hon. Are you all ri—"

"Get away from me, Grandma."

Which shouldn't bother me. Doesn't. I stay right where I am as she rips open the rainfly and her so-called friends gather her in. Leaving me to stand right where I am. Where I'll be if she needs me. Or doesn't. A wall they can bang on. Forget was there. Sleep near.

One last role I've realized I've come to like, or at least believe in.

CFK has a different approach. *"Out!"* I hear him snarl from all the way across the camp. "Get out. All of you!"

Inside the pussycat tent, flashlights switch off and whispers drop low. Mostly, that's so they can listen to CFK, but they also know I'm still here. They're waiting for me to walk away. They won't know when I do.

I allow myself a small smile, by myself in the dark. My husband gone. My long-ago regional theater life, such as it was, even more gone. The few faculty friends I've made in a quarter century of my second career retired, one by one. The hundreds of students I've loved and laughed with scattered into their lives, never looking back, and why should they?

"Nope," I hear CFK snap. "Did I say you could get dressed? Put it back."

Meaning everything, I realize. Pants. Shoes. He's got all four asshole boys out of their tents, standing barefoot at attention in the desert cold in their underwear. Laughter flickers across a few of their faces but dies fast. A fire that won't catch. Behind them, the night shadows have reached the base of the rock wall. Started across the sand.

I dig my hands into my pockets. It's his show. But those boys should be in their tents. Us, too. It bothers me that I can no longer hear him, and I lean forward. Consider going over there, but for all kinds of reasons, I stay put. Stand sentinel over this tent, and keep these girls inside it. This night needs no additional accelerant.

I'm not even sure CFK is talking anymore, and he doesn't seem to be moving, either. He, too, knows how to stand still, though he uses stillness differently. Teaching strategies, I have learned, are like martial arts disciplines, and we all pretty much subscribe to one form or another. Some are primarily about defense. Some—like mine, I hope— are for centering, locating qi. Some are for control, which can look and feel an awful lot like attack. Sometimes, it is.

Under our feet, the ground shudders again, the flash on the horizon beating the muffled *boom* to our senses as the bomb drops and the mountains twitch like images on an old antenna tv. Settle again, or don't, quite.

CFK has released the boys. Which is a relief. He's not coming back, yet, though. Is lurking outside tents, absolutely still, same as I am (except not quite. I hope. Guarding vs. stalking. Different disciplines).

Abruptly, I whirl, gaze flashing over flat sand toward the rocks. Shadows seem to slide off them, go still the split second before I catch them at it. Then I'm staring at my feet, thinking *snake, scorpion*.

What I see is my feet in sneakers in sand in moonlight. As though I'm standing on a beach at the lip of an ocean of shadow. Ghost of an ocean. Of the ooze we all crawled out of, evaporating now as our climate shifts and our age ends.

That first year—the Steph year—we had campfires every night, and the kids wanted ghost stories. We had a woman, then, an art teacher, young and Indian and beautiful and strange. Subscriber to the mesmerize-them teaching discipline. Hardest to maintain, at least once you're out of your twenties. She told a long, truly unsettling tale about hiking the perimeter of the Bloody Lake on the Northern Ridge in New Delhi, and dead children following her. It kept us all spellbound for a good fifteen minutes, and the adults for another ten. Then our students just wanted s'mores, and to throw graham crackers at each other. We let them wander back to their tents piecemeal. At the end—heat on my face, cold on my back, living children everywhere around me and the empty, black desert beyond—I asked Steph if there were any good Joshua Tree ghost stories. To my surprise, she smiled, looked young. Younger even than our art teacher. Barely older than my students. She probably was.

"Not that I've heard, believe it or not. No good ones. There's just not that much alive out here. Or that ever was alive. And the things that do die here die quietly. Or…"

That was the end of the smile. And the looking young. Instead of a ghost story, she told us about a tent full of dead migrant laborers the rangers had found a few months back. And then about a girl she'd known in Twentynine Palms whose mother had been gang-raped by Marines and left out here. The Marines got caught, confessed, tried to show police where they'd dumped her body. But she'd never been found.

That was also the night Steph showed me the disappearing trick. Stood up, shook herself hard as though exorcizing her own thoughts, motioned me to stand, and pulled me away from the firelight into the shadows. She told me to look right at her. Held still. Slid right.

The pussycat girls, I realize, have gone silent. Not only quiet but still. Possibly, they're sleeping. *How long have I been standing here?*

Too long. The cold isn't just creeping up my sleeves or under my scarf and hat; it's gotten inside. I'm about to yell to CFK to let the damn boys back in their sleeping bags when I realize he already has. He's just standing, too, ankle-deep in shadows, still and prickly as a barrel cactus. I'm tired. I don't want to be out here anymore. I want my tent and my air mattress—I got it to discourage scorpion climbing, not for glampy comfort, though that's not a distinction any real desert adventurer would recognize—and my little hooded camping lantern and my book. My earplugs so I won't hear my colleagues snoring, though I hate wearing those because then I can't hear the wind, either. Or the desert quiet.

I almost leave CFK to finish up. But he waves and trots back over. We meet at the flag line.

"All clear," I say, a little more firmly than I believe, and CFK holds up a finger.

We wait. Cold vibrates inside me, as though I'm a cave and *it* the living thing. I can almost hear it calling to itself in there. Sounding echoes. I'm watching the shadows all around the camp, which is why I actually see the shooting star this time, less a single streak than a scatter, like a thrown sparkler that flashes surprisingly low over the ridge to our east and then winks out all at once.

Sucking in a breath, I make myself *be here*. Remind myself to be. Cold, dark, kids, sand, crawling things, flying things, *no* things. Emptiness. Joe memories. That stupid song we danced to at his father's third wedding. *Uh-huh uh-huh uh-huh*. Only words I remember or need to remember.

"Okay," says CFK. "All clear."

We get maybe five steps from each other toward our own tents before the shrieking erupts.

It's right on top of us, and even as I'm ducking, hands flying to my head to ward off talons, I realize what it is. CFK does, too, or should; he had to have been here when we heard it last. But of course his first thought is that it's students, and he's whirling all over himself like that cartoon Tasmanian devil, eyes everywhere, legs crouched for the lurch. He figures it out a few seconds after I do. Straightens, and I straighten, get my hands back down by my sides. I shrug. Smile at him. What else is there to do?

"Goddamn it," he mutters, right as the kids start sticking heads out again. "Get back in!" he yells, but it's whack-a-mole, hopeless, and will be until the concert is over. So I just listen.

Another shriek, then a long moan. A breath. Six or seven staccato shrieks, not quite in a pattern, but then another bomb rumbles the earth, and for a few seconds, it really is like music, some contemporary Morton Feldman-type thing, little blips or bursts of sound, long silences. The sounds nearly falling into rhythms, falling apart. Drifting out of phase.

"Do you remember this story?" I say to CFK. Even I don't know if I'm calming or provoking him. Either way, it's a sort of fun. A way not to be annoyed or bored or even cold.

"I remember this *guy.*"

I glance sidelong at him. "You actually saw him? I thought even the rangers didn't know who it was."

"I know who it was. That fucking beard. You need a beard that long to hide a smirk that deep."

Amazingly, I know who he means. Of all the bearded park service personnel we've spent time with out here, that guy liked himself most. And the kids least. Tom, I think.

But Tom was not the Naked Flautist. Was way too resentful of the imposition work placed on his time to want to entertain teenagers, or wow them, or even scare them.

The Naked Flautist. Who crawls up the rocks some starlit nights, flings off his clothes, screws together his instrument, and lets fly. Not a ghost story, exactly. Not even a story. But effective for keeping certain kinds of kids *off* the rocks. Or luring others on. Or making a whole camp groan and laugh. Or, just sometimes, triggering awe all over again in the middle of the Nothing in the middle of the night.

It's already over, I realize. A shooting star of a Naked Flautist show. There and gone.

The hooting starts. On the girls' side, for once, the pussycat tent, and I sigh as hoots break out all over our camp, from every corner. Like freaked out chimps, I'm thinking, except less wild than that. Stupider. Its only intention communal disruption, not warning.

"*God*damn it," says CFK, and he hurtles straight through the boys' area toward the asshole tent.

With a sigh, I pocket my hands, start toward the pussycats. But I stop when I see Jayna poking out of her tent, staring up at the rocks. Her blunt-cut, dyed-red hair all over the place, like kicked embers. Tears in her eyes.

Tears.

"You okay, sweetie?" I say. I consider crouching, but don't want to draw other kids' attention to her. She's alone in there, I remember. Parental request. She still gets too nervous to sleep near others.

I try following her gaze, but all that's up there is ridge and shadow. From the boys' side, I hear Fletcher or one of his cronies shouting, "We didn't even do anything!"

Followed by CFK's snarl. "Well, you're not going to, now."

Like rams rutting. For whom, and to what end?

The stars go out.

Have been out? How long has it been this dark? Is that *what Jayna's looking at?*

Of course it is.

"Ms. J," she whispers, and I want to shush her, slip her a tissue, remind her that she has classmates all around and pussycat predators ten feet away and laughing, though probably not at her. At least not yet. "It's so deep."

I'm half into my crouch, hand reaching to wipe her cheek, the obvious question on my lips when Fletcher screams, "OW! *You fucking bit me!*"

Just like that, I'm sprinting across the sand in precisely the way twenty years of instructions from rangers have warned not to. All around me, kids are out of their tents, blinking in the lack of light. They look grayed, two-dimensional. *Vulnerable.* No prickers or stingers or stink-glands to keep them safe.

Everything here is trying to kill you.

"Kerber, get away from that tent," I'm shouting, but even as I do, I see, and in my panic, I pull up too fast, almost tumbling into the cactus that's twitching like a Venus fly trap right next to me. It has blooms on it. In the gloom the blooms look gray, like stars this thing has caught and webbed.

From the place *he* stopped—a good ten feet from Fletcher's tent, nowhere near biting distance—CFK hunches by a mesquite bush, hands up in a sort of wrestler's crouch. He's swaying slightly, which has the effect of making him look rooted. Part of the plant. Like a yucca stalk.

Like the rangers around the rattlesnake bush this morning, after they realized Mama had come home.

"Okay, guys," he's saying. "Slowly, okay? One at a time. Move away from there. Away from the tent. Toward me."

And the kids, the asshole boys—who are just boys, for at least a little longer—they're doing exactly what he says. One at a time.

"Look at me!" CFK snaps. "At *me*."

One by one, they come, almost tiptoeing. But fast. As though evacuating a crashed plane. As they reach CFK, every single one glances back. Only when the last reaches him do I realize Fletcher isn't with them.

That his tent is rippling.

That there are noises coming from it.

For one moment, CFK swings around. His eyes grab mine. His face is half-obscured by shadow. By *these* shadows. Even so, I finally see what I should have years ago. Have always seen but never recognized.

Crazy Fucking Kerber is afraid. He Is always afraid.

"Stay there," I call. "Kerber, wait. I'm…" But the rest dies in my mouth.

Beyond him, Fletcher's tent has swelled. It's not billowing, not even ballooning. Just…shoving outward. Like the neck of an anaconda with a rat in it.

I stumble forward, but way too slow. CFK has already spun back that way, and he's seen. Then he's diving headlong for the tent. He rips at its still-zipped front, tearing it open, and there's a *wetness* to that sound, like tendons being severed, and then he's through. Inside.

Gone.

Instinctively, I dart sideways, not toward the tent mouth, which *stinks* even from here like the chemical toilet, except minus chemicals. Like the raw, rotting insides of us. "Help me," I'm shouting to the boys. To any kids who will listen.

A shocking, marvelous number of them do. Immediately, without hesitation. Three of them right there with me, hurtling across the sand. "The tent," I'm shouting, not making sense even to myself, but somehow the kids understand. They always understand, so much more than we think or is good for them.

Even as the canvas bells out to meet them, two start ripping at the rain fly, peeling it free. The rest drop to their knees around me, digging at the stone-hard sand in all four corners. Grabbing the metal spikes, which should be freezing but instead are warm. Not in and of themselves, I realize. More *bathed* in warmth. Bones in blood.

"*Pull!*" I'm shouting as the tent flaps, leans way over sideways (in wind, just wind), snaps straight, and there are voices in there, just the two, "Get off, get it off!" and "CFK, FUCK!". Hands over mine, seemingly becoming mine, and we're yanking, straining. The peg pops free of the ground. Seconds later, they're all out, and for one horrific second, the tent seems to lift off the desert floor like a magic carpet. Or a bloated dragonfly.

Then it sags to the ground and lets Fletcher and CFK go.

Spits them out.

That's what it looks like. That's what it was. I know, already, that I will always think so.

We're staring at each other. All of us. The pussycat girls, so many girls over here where they're not allowed. Fletcher's tentmates and their peers who hate them and their peers who are just other kids who happened to be in their class on this trip on this night on this day when the snakes and shadows came to camp. When the desert finally noticed us.

In a surprisingly short time—less than an hour, I don't even remember anyone breaking off to use the toilet—we are all back in our tents. Even CFK and me. I do ask, one time, what he thinks happened.

For answer, he looks at me. The look I now recognize. But he gives the CFK shrug. "When?"

We don't realize, of course, until the next morning. No one does. Not even the kids in the tents around her. That's the worst part. It doesn't even seem possible unless you've been out there. When I ask the rest of them later, after every single tent is down and packed except hers, whether it occurred to anyone to check on her, or to come ask one of us, the other girls just say they figured she'd gotten up early, gone for a dawn walk. Seemed like something she would do.

Which is true enough. I'd seen her do it earlier in the trip. We'd seen each other out there, walking the dawn. Waved but left one another alone.

Jayna.

I don't cry while I'm still with the kids. There isn't time. First, we have to do the frantic search, all day, in heat that suddenly roars in from the open Mojave and envelops the rangers, police, everyone. Then there are calls to the school to make, the helpless attempts at explanation which sound pathetic even to us. Because what do we even know?

That they came in a pack? Whatever they were? One group distracting us at Fletcher's tent while the other...

Is that even what I think? Because like Steph said. Every single thing out there...

Finally, in the end, there's nothing left but the drive home to my empty house, to sit on my porch and stare helplessly over the tops of the city lights, through the silhouettes of the San Gabriels toward the nothingness beyond. The Nothing that Lives. And Preys. And, like any proper predator, takes the ones from the back. The weakest and smallest. The ones who are alone.

CEMETERY DANCE PUBLICATIONS
PAPERBACKS AND EBOOKS!

THE DISMEMBERED
by Jonathan Janz

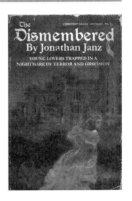

In the spring of 1912, American writer Arthur Pearce is reeling from the wounds inflicted by a disastrous marriage. But his plans to travel abroad, write a new novel, and forget about his ex-wife are interrupted by a lovely young woman he encounters on a London-bound train. Her name is Sarah Coyle, and the tale she tells him chills his blood....

"...a creepy, fast read embellished with supernatural elements and over-the-top characters... Readers nostalgic for past literature but in search of fresher reading material with more contemporary details will appreciate this addition to modern horror."

—*Booklist*

THE EATER OF GODS
by Dan Franklin

Dan Franklin's debut supernatural thriller is a tale of grief, of loneliness, and of an ageless, hungry fury that waits with ready tooth and claw beneath the sand.

"This neat little book, Franklin's debut, is much fresher than its B-movie premise might suggest. Franklin is a horror writer to watch."

—*Publishers Weekly*

IN THE PORCHES OF MY EARS
by Norman Prentiss

LEAN CLOSER. Let these stories whisper poison into your ears...

"I've never forgotten a Norman Prentiss story. He builds his nightmares gently, word by word, sentence by sentence, working his way into your subconscious so that you are never sure again if it happened to you, or you dreamt it, or it was a Prentiss story."

—Kaaron Warren, Award-Winning author of *Through Splintered Walls*